WITHDRAWN

In the Labyrinth

By the same author

THE ERASERS   *a novel*
THE VOYEUR   *a novel*
JEALOUSY   *a novel*
SNAPSHOTS *and* TOWARDS A NEW NOVEL   *shorter fiction and Criticism*
LAST YEAR IN MARIENBAD   *a cine-novel*

in preparation
THE HOUSE OF ASSIGNATION   *a novel*
THE IMMORTAL ONE   *a cine-novel*

In the Labyrinth

a novel by

Alain Robbe-Grillet

translated by
Christine Brooke-Rose

CALDER AND BOYARS · LONDON

First published 1959 in France as *Dans Le Labyrinthe*
© 1959 Les Editions De Minuit

This translation first published 1967
by Calder and Boyars Ltd.,
18 Brewer St. London, W.1.

© 1967 Calder and Boyars Ltd.

PRINTED IN GREAT BRITAIN BY
NORTHUMBERLAND PRESS LIMITED
GATESHEAD

This story is fiction, not a report. It describes a reality which is not necessarily that of the reader's own experience: thus the infantry in the French army does not have the military number on the coat-collar. Similarly, the recent history of Western Europe has recorded no important battle at Reichenfels or even nearby. And yet the reality here in question is strictly physical, that is to say it has no allegorical significance. The reader should therefore see in it only the objects, the gestures, the words and the events that are told, without seeking to give them either more or less meaning than they would have in his own life, or in his own death.

A.R-G.

I AM alone here now, safe and sheltered. Outside it is raining, outside in the rain one has to walk with head bent, hand shielding eyes that peer ahead nevertheless, a few yards ahead, a few yards of wet asphalt; outside it is cold, the wind blows between the bare black branches; the wind blows among the leaves, sweeping whole boughs into a swaying motion, swaying, swaying, that throws its shadow on the white roughcast of the walls. Outside the sun is shining, there is not a tree, not a bush to give shade, one has to walk in the full sunlight, hand shielding eyes that look ahead, a few yards ahead only, a few yards of dusty asphalt where the wind traces parallels, curves and spirals.

Here the sun does not enter, nor does the wind, nor the rain, nor the dust. The fine dust that dulls the shine of the horizontal planes, the varnished tabletop, the polished parquet, the marble of the mantelpiece and that of the chest of drawers, the cracked marble of the chest of drawers, the only

7

dust here comes from the room itself: from the gaps in the parquet possibly, or from the bed, or the curtains, or the ashes in the fireplace.

On the varnished tabletop the dust has marked the place occupied for a while—for a few hours, a few days, minutes, weeks—by small objects since removed, the bases of which are clearly outlined for a while longer, a circle, a square, a rectangle, other less simple forms, some of them partly overlapping, already blurred or half erased as if by the flick of a rag.

When the outline is precise enough for the shape to be definitely identified the original object can easily be found not far away. Thus the circular shape has obviously been left by a glass ashtray now placed just beside it. Similarly, away on its own, the square in the far left-hand corner of the table corresponds to the base of a copper lamp now standing at the right-hand corner: a square base about an inch high, topped by a disc of the same thickness bearing at its centre a fluted column.

The lampshade projects a circle of light on to the ceiling. But this circle is not complete: on one side it is cut at ceiling level by the wall, the wall behind the table. This wall, unlike the other three which are entirely papered, is hidden from top to bottom and across most of its width by thick red curtains made of some heavy, velvety material.

Outside it is snowing. The wind drives the fine dry crystals over the dark asphalt of the pavement, and with each gust the crystals fall in white lines, parallels, curves, spirals, no sooner disrupted than they are again taken up in whirls, chased round at ground level, now suddenly immobilised again, forming renewed spirals, scrolls, forked undulations, arabesques in motion, and then again disrupted. One has to walk with head further bent, hand firmer on the brow to protect eyes that can only just see a few inches of ground in front of the feet, a few inches of grizzled white where the feet appear, one after the other, withdrawing, one after the other, alternately.

But the staccato sound of metallic heels on the asphalt, approaching steadily along the rectilinear street, ringing out more and more clearly in the dead calm of the frozen night, the sound of heels cannot reach this place, nor can any other noise from the outside. The street is too long, the curtains too thick, the house too high. No noise, not even muffled, ever penetrates the walls of the room, no vibration, no breath of air, and in the silence minute particles float slowly down, hardly visible in the light from the lampshade, gently down, vertically, always at the same speed, and the fine grey dust settles in an even layer on the parquet floor, the counterpane, the furniture.

Across the polished floor the felt slippers have traced gleaming paths, from the bed to the chest of drawers, from the chest of drawers to the fireplace, from the fireplace to the table. And, on the table,

9

the removal of objects has also disturbed the continuity of the dust-film which, more or less thick according to the age of the surfaces, has here and there been interrupted altogether: a square of varnished wood, as sharp as if drawn with a ruler, occupies the rear left-hand corner of the table, not in the angle itself but parallel to the edges, about four inches from them. The square itself measures some six by six inches. The wood, reddish brown, shines there, almost untouched by dust.

To the right a simple shape, more blurred, already covered by several days' deposit, is nevertheless still discernible; at a certain angle it acquires sufficient clarity for its outline to be followed without too much difficulty. It is a kind of cross: an elongated main shape, like a table knife but wider, coming to a point at one end and slightly swollen at the other, cut across by a much shorter cross-piece consisting of two flame-shaped projections laid out symmetrically on either side of the main axis, just at the base of the swollen part, that is to say at about a third of the total length. It looks like a flower, the swollen end representing a long closed corolla, at the end of a stem, with two small lateral leaves below it. Or it could be a vaguely human figurine: an oval head, two very short arms, and the body ending in a point below. Or even a dagger, with a hilt separating the handle from the stout, blunt-ended, double-edged blade.

Still further to the left following the direction of

the flower's tail or the dagger's point, a circle, hardly blurred at all, is just broached on one side by a second circle of the same size, but consisting of more than just a projection on the table: the glass ashtray. Then come a few uncertain lines, criss-crossing, left no doubt by various papers, moved several times in such a way as to blur the pattern, very clear in places, or on the contrary veiled by the grizzled film, and elsewhere more than half erased as if by the flick of a rag.

Beyond them stands the lamp, in the right-angle of the table: a base six by six inches square, a disc of the same diameter, a fluted column bearing a dark and very slightly conical lampshade. On the upper circle of the lampshade a fly is moving slowly, continuously, projecting on the ceiling a distorted shadow in which no element of the initial insect is recognisable: neither wings, nor body, nor legs; the whole has become a single filiform stroke, a regular dotted line, unclosed, like a hexagon with a missing side: the image of the glowing filament in the electric bulb. At one of its angles this small open polygon touches the inside edge of the vast circle of light produced by the lamp. It moves slowly but continuously all round the circumference. When it reaches the angle of the wall and ceiling it disappears into the folds of the heavy red curtain.

Outside it is snowing. Outside it has snowed, it was snowing, outside it is snowing. The massed flakes descend gently, their fall steady, uninter-

rupted, vertical—for there is not a breath of wind—
in front of the high grey houses, preventing a clear
view of their façades, the alignment of the roofs, the
positions of the doors and windows. There must
be rows of identical, regular windows repeated at
every level from one end to the other of the
rectilinear street.

An intersection, at right-angles, shows another
entirely similar street: the same roadway without
traffic, the same high, grey houses, the same closed
windows, the same deserted pavements. At the corner of the pavement a street-lamp is alight, although
it is broad daylight. But the daylight is without
brightness, making everything look flat and dull. Instead of the spectacular perspectives which these
rows of houses ought to display, there is only a mean-
ingless criss-crossing of lines, and the snow that falls
continuously, removing all depth from the landscape
as if this blurred view were a badly painted *trompe
l'oeil* on a flat wall.

In the angle of the wall and ceiling the shadow
of the fly, a blown-up image of the filament in the
electric bulb, reappears and continues on its journey around the edge of the white circle violently lit
by the lamp. Its speed is still the same: feeble and
constant. In the dark zone extending to the left a
spot of light stands out, corresponding to a small
round hole in the dark parchment of the lampshade; it is not precisely a spot but a thin dotted
line, unclosed, a regular hexagon with a missing

12

side: a further enlarged image, this time fixed, from the same luminous source, the same glowing filament.

It is again the same filament, that of an identical lamp, or one hardly larger, which is shining uselessly at the crossing of the two streets, enclosed in its glass cage at the top of a cast-iron column, an old-fashioned ornate gaslamp converted to electricity.

Thin stalks of stylised ivy, cast in the metal, twist round the cast-iron pedestal's conical base, which widens out towards the bottom, in several more or less prominent rings: wavy stems, palmate leaves with five pointed lobes and five very visible veins where the black paint is chipped off, revealing the rusted metal. A little higher a hip, an arm, a shoulder lean against the shaft of the lamp-post. The man is wearing an army coat of doubtful hue, faded to somewhere between green and khaki. His face is greyish; the features are drawn, giving an impression of extreme fatigue; but perhaps a beard of more than one day's growth is the chief cause of this impression. The prolonged wait, the prolonged immobility in the cold may also have drained the colour from the cheeks, the brow, the lips.

The eyelids are grey, like the rest; they are lowered. The head is bent forward. The eyes are looking down towards the ground, that is towards the edge of the snow-covered pavement, a little beyond the foot of the lamp-post and the two large, round-toed boots made of coarse leather full of

13

scratches, dents and various other marks more or less covered over with black shoepolish. The layer of snow is hardly thick enough to sink visibly beneath the feet, so that the soles of the boots rest —as near as makes no difference—at the level of the white surface that surrounds them. At the edge of the pavement this surface is unblemished, without brightness but lying evenly, intact, finely dotted in its original grain. A little snow has accumulated on the upper part of the last raised ring around the flared base of the lamp-post, forming a white circle above the black circle where the lamp-post meets the ground. Higher up, some snow has caught also on other irregularities of the cone, emphasising in white the successive rings and the upper contours of the ivy-leaves, as well as the fragments of stalk and the horizontal or slightly inclined veins.

But the bottom of the coat has swept away a few of these small deposits, just as the boots in their several changes of position have produced small piles of snow around them, leaving some yellower spaces here and there, half-lifted harder pieces and the deep marks of nailheads in quincunx patterns. By the chest of drawers the felt slippers have traced a large bright zone in the dust, and another by the table, just where there ought to be a desk-seat or a chair, a stool, something or other to sit on. Between the two they have traced a narrow path of gleaming parquet; another path goes from the table to the bed. Parallel with the houses, a little nearer to them

14

than to the gutter of the street, a rectilinear path also defines the snow-covered pavement. Yellow-grey in colour, from the trampling feet of people now gone, it passes between the lighted street-lamp and the door of the last building, then turns at right-angles and continues up the perpendicular street, still alongside the houses, about a third of the way across the width of the pavement, along its whole length.

Then another path begins, going from the bed to the chest of drawers. From there, the narrow band of bright parquet leading from the chest of drawers to the table, joining the two large dust-free circles, curves slightly to pass nearer the fireplace, the shutter of which is raised, disclosing a heap of ashes, with no fire-dogs. The black marble of the mantelpiece, like everything else, is covered with grey dust. But the layer is less thick there than on the table or on the floor, and it is uniform over the whole surface of the ledge; no object stands there now and only one has left its trace, clear and black in the very centre of the rectangle. It is the same four-branched cross: one branch long and pointed, one shorter and oval continuing the first, and two very small ones shaped like flames placed perpendicularly on either side.

A similar motif still can be seen on the wallpaper. The paper is pale grey, with vertical stripes that are hardly darker; between the darker stripes, in the middle of the lighter bands, rises a line of small designs, all identical, in a very dark grey: a floret, a kind of clove, or a minute flaming torch, the handle of which makes up what was just now the dagger blade, the handle of that dagger now representing the flame, and the two flame-shaped lateral pieces which were then the dagger's hilt this time forming the shallow cup that prevents burning matter from flowing down the handle.

But it could perhaps rather be a sort of electric torch, for the apex of what is supposed to produce light is clearly rounded, like an elongated bulb, instead of being pointed like a flame. The motif, reproduced some thousands of times up and down the walls all round the room, is a simplified silhouette of a large insect, uniformly coloured so that it is difficult to interpret: in particular no relief is discernible, any more than is the glowing filament which must be inside the bulb. In any case the bulb is hidden by the lampshade. Only the image of the filament is visible on the ceiling: a small interrupted hexagon luminously outlined on the shaded area, and further to the right another small hexagon, identical but moving, thrown as in a shadow-show on the circle of light projected by the lamp, moving slowly, regularly, round the inside of the curve, until the moment when, at the angle of the wall and ceiling, it disappears.

The soldier is carrying a parcel under his left arm. His right arm, from shoulder to elbow, leans against the lamp-post. His head is turned towards the street, showing the ill-shaven beard and the army number on the collar of the coat, five or six black figures within a red lozenge. Behind him the door of the corner house is not quite closed—not ajar either, but with the leaf that opens just pushed against the narrower, fixed leaf, leaving a gap of perhaps an inch or two, a vertical strip of darkness. To the right is the row of ground-floor windows, uninterrupted except by the doors of each building, identical windows and identical doors, the doors themselves fairly similar to the windows in shape and in dimension. Not a single shop can be seen from one end of the street to the other.

To the left of the door with the ill-fitting leaves there are only two windows, then the quoin of the house, then perpendicularly a new succession of identical windows and doors, like images of the first, as if a mirror had been set up there, forming an obtuse angle (a right-angle plus half a right-angle) with the plane of the houses; and the same series is repeated: two windows, a door, four windows, a door, etc. . . . The first door is slightly open on a dark corridor, its two unequal leaves leaving a black gap just wide enough for a man to slip through, or at least a child.

In front of the door, at the pavement's edge, a street-lamp is alight although it is still daylight. But in the diffuse dullness of this snowy landscape the light of the electric bulb stands out at first glance; a little brighter, a little yellower, a little more precise. A soldier is leaning against the lamp-post, bare-headed, his face down, his two hands hidden in the pockets of his coat. Under his right arm he has a brown paper parcel, something like a shoebox, with a piece of white string tied no doubt in a cross; but the only part of the string that is visible goes round the box lengthwise, the other part, if it exists, being hidden by the coat sleeve, on which, at elbow-level, are several dark smears that could be traces of fresh mud, or paint, or grease.

The box wrapped in brown paper is now lying on the chest of drawers. The white string has gone, and the wrapping paper, tidily folded back on the short side of the oblong box, is gaping slightly like an open beak, very precise in form, pointing obliquely downwards. At this precise spot in the marble of the chest of drawers there is a long crack, more straight than winding, which passes diagonally under the corner of the box and reaches the wall at the centre of the chest-top. Immediately above hangs the picture.

The picture framed in varnished wood, the striped wallpaper, the fireplace with the heap of ashes, the desk-table with its lamp and opaque lamp-shade and its glass ashtray, the heavy red curtains, the big divan covered with the same red velvety material, and then the chest with its three drawers, the cracked marble, the brown parcel lying on it and, higher up again the picture and the vertical lines of small grey insects climbing to the ceiling.

18

Outside the sky has the same heavy whiteness. It is still day. The street is deserted: no traffic on the road, no pedestrians on the pavements. It has been snowing; and the snow has not yet melted. It lies in a thinnish layer—two inches or so—but perfectly even, covering all horizontal surfaces with the same dull, neutral whiteness. The only marks than can be seen are the rectilinear paths, parallel to the rows of houses and to the gutters which are still quite visible (made even more distinct by the vertical edge of the pavement, which remains black), and dividing the pavements into two unequal bands along their entire length. At the crossroads, at the foot of a lamp-post, is a small circle of trampled snow with the same yellowish tinge as the narrow paths that skirt the houses. The doors are shut. The windows are empty of silhouettes, whether glued to the panes or outlined in the background in the depths of the rooms. In any case it would appear from the flatness of this whole décor that there is nothing behind these window-panes, behind these doors, behind these walls. And the whole scene remains empty: not a man, not a woman, not even a child.

The picture in its frame of varnished wood is of a café scene. It is a black and white engraving, dating from the last century, or a good reproduction. A large number of characters fills the whole scene: a crowd of customers, standing or sitting, and, on the far left, the proprietor, slightly elevated behind his counter.

The proprietor is a big, bald man wearing an apron. He is bending forward, both hands on the edge of the counter, leaning over the few half-empty glasses on it, his massive shoulders turned towards a small group of men in long jackets or frock coats, who seem to be taking part in a lively discussion; they are standing in various attitudes and most of them are making expansive gestures which in some cases even involve the whole body, and seem very expressive.

To the right, that is at the centre of the picture, several groups of drinkers are seated around tables which are irregularly placed in or rather crammed into a space too small to contain such a crowd with comfort. These too are making exaggerated gestures and violent facial contortions, but their movements, like their expressions, are frozen by the drawing, stopped, interrupted, cut short in mid-performance, and this has the additional effect of making their meaning very uncertain; all the more so since the words that are gushing out on every side have been, as it were, absorbed by a thick glass partition. Some of the characters, carried away by passion, are half-rising from their chairs or their benches, stretching out an arm above all those heads towards some speaker further away. Everywhere hands are raised, mouths open, torsos and necks twist round, fists clench, brought down on a table or shaken in the air.

On the extreme right a knot of men, nearly all dressed as workmen like those sitting at the tables, have their backs turned to the others and are crowding together to look at some notice or poster stuck on the wall. Towards the front, between these turned backs and the first row of drinkers facing the other way, a boy is squatting on the floor among the shapelessly trousered legs, among the clumsy shoes that are stamping about and trying to move towards the left; he is partly protected on the other side by the bench. The child is seen full face. He is sitting with both legs folded beneath him; and both his arms are wrapped round a big box, something like a shoebox. Nobody is paying any attention to him. Perhaps he has been knocked down in some scuffle or other. Not far from there, moreover, in the foreground, a chair is lying on the floor, knocked over.

A little apart, as if separated from the surrounding crowd by the unoccupied area—a narrow one, certainly, but sufficient nevertheless for their isolation to be apparent; sufficient at any rate to mark them out despite their background position—three soldiers, sitting at a smaller table, the last but one on the right towards the back, contrast strongly in their stiffness and immobility with the civilians who fill the room. The soldiers are looking straight ahead, resting their hands on a sort of chequered oilcloth; they have no glasses in front of them. And they alone are wearing hats—forage caps with short points. Right at the back the full tables merge more or less with the people standing in a fairly confused muddle where, in any case, the drawing is more vague. Below the engraving, in the white border, a caption is inscribed in an Italian hand : 'The Defeat at Reichenfels'.

On further scrutiny the isolation of the three soldiers seems to result less from the minimal space between them and the crowd than from the direction of the surrounding gazes. The background silhouettes all seem to be making their way—or trying to make their way, for the passage is difficult —towards the left of the picture, where there is perhaps a door (though this hypothetical exit cannot be seen on the drawing, because of a row of coat-stands overloaded with hats and clothes); the faces are looking ahead (that is, towards the coat-stands), except one here and there that is turned to speak to someone behind. The dense crowd on the right is looking solely in the direction of the right wall. The drinkers at the tables face quite naturally, in each circle, towards the centre of the group, or else towards a neighbour, whether immediate or not. As for the men at the counter, they too are interested only in their own conversation, into which the proprietor is leaning forward, taking no notice of his other customers. Among the different groups many isolated characters are moving about, not yet settled, but obviously intending to take up quite soon one or other of the attitudes available: to go and look at the posters, to sit at one of the tables, or else to make their way behind the coat-stands; one look at them is enough to tell that each has already decided on his next occupation; not one of their faces, any more than those within the groups, shows any trace of hesitation, puzzlement, interior struggle or self-preoccupation. The three soldiers, on the other hand, seem lost. They are not talking among themselves; they show no interest in anything in particular: neither posters, nor drinks, nor neighbours. They have nothing to do. Nobody is looking at them, and they have nothing to look at themselves. The direction of their faces—one full, the other in profile, the third half in profile—indicates no common object of attention. In fact the first, the only one whose features are wholly visible, is staring with fixed, empty eyes devoid of all expression.

The contrast between the three soldiers and the crowd is further emphasised by a clarity of outline, a precision, a minuteness much more marked than for the other characters on the same plane. The artist has depicted them with as much attention to detail and almost as much strength of line as if they had been sitting in the foreground. But the composition is so crammed that this is at first unnoticeable. The full face in particular has been drawn with a finical care that seems to bear no relation to the void of feeling it is made to express. No thought can be read there. The face is simply exhausted, on the thin side, and made to look thinner still by a beard unshaven for several days. This thinness, these shadows that sharpen the features without thereby revealing the slightest individuality, nevertheless bring out the brightness of the wide-open eyes.

The military coat is buttoned to the collar, where the army number can be seen on each side, mounted on an inlaid lozenge. The forage cap is set squarely on the head entirely hiding the hair which, judging by the temples, is close-cropped. The man is sitting stiffly with his hands flat on the table, which is covered with a red and white chequered oilcloth.

He has long finished his drink. He does not seem to be thinking of leaving. And yet, around him, the last customers have left the café. The light is dim, the proprietor having turned off most of the lamps before himself leaving the room.

The soldier, his eyes wide open, continues to stare into the shadows before him, a few yards before him, where the child is standing, also stiff and motionless, arms hanging down his body. But it is as if the soldier cannot see the child—neither the child nor anything else. He appears to have fallen asleep from exhaustion, sitting there at the table, his eyes wide open.

It is the child who utters the first words. He says: 'Are you asleep?' He has spoken very low, as if afraid to wake the sleeper. The latter has not

24

moved. After a few seconds the child repeats, hardly any louder:

'Are you asleep?' And he adds in the same neutral, slightly sing-song voice: 'You can't sleep there, you know.'

The soldier has not moved. The child might think he is alone in the room, that he is only playing at conversation with someone who does not exist, or with a doll, a dummy who cannot reply. In which case it would indeed have been useless to speak louder; the voice was already that of a child telling himself a story.

But the voice has stopped, as if giving up the unequal struggle against the silence, which now settles once again. Perhaps the child also has fallen asleep.

'No . . . Yes . . . I know,' the soldier says.

Neither of them has moved. The child is still standing in the shadow, arms hanging down his body. He has not even seen the man's lips move. The man is sitting at the table under the only bulb left burning in the room; his head has not given the slightest nod, his eyes have not even blinked; and his mouth remains shut.

'Your father . . .' says the soldier. Then he stops. But this time the lips have moved slightly.

'He's not my father,' says the child.

And he turns his head towards the black rectangle of the glazed door.

Outside it is snowing. The small, massed flakes

have begun falling again on the white road. The wind that is now blowing drives them horizontally so that one has to walk with head bent, with head a little more bent, hand firmer on the brow to protect eyes that can only just see a few square inches of crunchy snow, not very thick, hardened already by the trampling of feet. At the crossroads the soldier hesitates, looks for the sign that should tell him the name of this transverse street. But in vain: the blue enamel plaques are missing, or too high up, and the night is too dark; and the small, massed flakes soon blind anyone who persists in looking up. Besides a street-name would hardly provide him with any useful information in this town which he does not know.

He hesitates a little longer, looks ahead once more and then behind him, the way he has just come, down the road punctuated by the electric lamps the lights of which, closer and closer together, less and less bright, vanish quickly in the murky night. Then he turns right into the perpendicular street, also deserted, edged with identical houses, and with the same succession of widely but regularly spaced lamp-posts, their meagre light catching the snowflakes in their slanting fall.

The white dots, falling fast and close together, all at once change direction; they trace vertical lines for a few moments, then quickly readopt a position close to the horizontal. Then they freeze to a sudden standstill and, with a swift veering of the wind, begin rushing the opposite way, falling at an equally shallow angle which they give up abruptly to resume their previous route, once again forming parallel, almost horizontal lines that cross the illuminated area from left to right, towards the unlighted windows.

On the window-sills the snow has piled up in an uneven layer, very thin on the rim of the ledge, thicker at the back, and forming on the right an already considerable mass which fills the corner and comes up to the pane. All the ground-floor windows, one after the other, show exactly the same amount of snow piling up to the right in the same way.

At the next crossroads, under the lamp at the corner of the pavement, a child has stopped. He is half-hidden by the cast-iron column, the thicker base of which in fact wholly conceals the lower part of his body. He is looking towards the approaching soldier. He does not seem put out by the storm, or by the snow that patches his black clothes with white, both his cape and his beret. He is about ten years old, and has an attentive expression. His head turns with the soldier's advance, his eyes following him as he reaches the lamp-post then passes it. As the soldier is walking slowly, the child has time to scrutinise him carefully from top to toe: the ill-shaven cheeks, the visible exhaustion, the soiled and crumpled army coat, the sleeves devoid of stripes, the parcel in its wet paper held under his left arm, the two hands buried in the pockets, the puttees wound hastily, irregularly, the back of the right boot showing a gash at least four inches long on the upper and the heel, which looks deep enough to have penetrated the thickness of the leather; and yet the boot is not split open and the gash has simply been rubbed over with black polish, so that it now looks the same dark grey as the undamaged part of the boot.

The man has stopped. Without moving the rest of his body he has turned his head back towards the child who is looking at him, three steps away already, streaked already with innumerable white lines.

After a moment the soldier slowly pivots and moves tentatively towards the lamp-post. The boy steps back a little, against the iron pedestal; at the same time he draws the flaps of his cape together, holding them from inside without his hands showing. The man has stopped. Now the gusts of snow no longer hit him full in the face and he can hold his head up without too much difficulty.

'Don't be afraid,' he says.

He takes another step towards the child and says again, a little louder: 'Don't be afraid.'

The child does not reply. Without appearing to feel the densely falling flakes which hardly even make him screw up his eyes, he continues to stare straight into the soldier's face. The soldier begins:

'Do you know where . . . ?'

But he does not continue. The question he was about to ask is not the right one. A veering of the wind once again whips the snow into his face. He draws his right hand from his coat pocket and holds it like a blinker against his temple. He has no gloves, his fingers are red and stained with grease. When the gust has died down he puts his hand back into his pocket.

'Where does it lead to that way?' he asks.

The boy still says nothing. His eyes have moved from the soldier to the end of the street, in the direction the man has just indicated with his head; he can see only the receding line of lights, getting closer and closer together, less and less bright, and disappearing in the night.

'Well? Are you afraid I'm going to eat you?'

'No,' says the child. 'I'm not afraid.'

'Well then, tell me where I get to that way.'

'I don't know,' says the child.

And he brings his eyes back towards this ill-dressed, unshaven soldier, who does not even know where he is going. Then, without warning, he turns suddenly, swings nimbly round the lamp-post and begins to run at full speed past the houses, back up the street down which the soldier has just come. In a moment he has vanished.

At the next lamp-post the electric light illuminates him for a few seconds; he is still running just as fast; the flaps of his cape are flying behind him. He

29

reappears once more, then a second time, then again at each lamp-post, then no more.

The soldier turns and continues on his way. The snow is now hitting him full in the face again.

He changes the parcel over to his right arm in order to try and protect his eyes with his left hand, on the side where the wind is blowing most continuously. But he quickly gives up and plunges his stiffened, frozen hand back into his coat pocket. And all he does, in order to get less snow in his eyes, is to turn his head downwards and to one side, towards the unlighted windows, where the white layer continues to deepen in the right-hand corner of the sill.

Yet it is this same boy, with the serious look, who led him to the café run by the man who is not his father. And it was a similar scene, under a lamp-post like this one, at an identical crossroads. Only the snow was perhaps falling a little less violently. The flakes were thicker, heavier, slower. But the boy answered just as reticently, hugging the flaps of his black cape against his legs. He had the same attentive expression, as impassive under the falling flakes. He hesitated as long, with each question, before giving his answer, which gave the questioner no enlightenment. Where did one get to that way? A long, silent gaze towards the unseen end of the road, then the calm voice:

'To the boulevard.'

'And that way?'

The boy slowly turns his eyes in the new direction the man has just indicated with his head. His features betray no sign of concentration and no uncertainty as he repeats in the same neutral tone:

'To the boulevard.'

'The same one?'

Silence again, and the snow falling, more and more heavy and slow.

'Yes,' says the boy. Then after a pause: 'No,' and finally with sudden violence: 'It's the boulevard!'

'And is it far?' the soldier asks.

The child is still looking at the receding line of lights, getting closer and closer together, less and less bright, which in that direction too disappear in the murky night.

'Yes,' he says, his voice now calm again, itself distant, as if elsewhere.

The soldier waits a moment longer in case a 'No' is to follow. But the boy is already running past the houses, down the track of hardened snow which the soldier took in the opposite direction a few minutes before. As the fugitive passes through the lighted area round a street-lamp, his dark cape flies widely around him for a few seconds, once, twice, three times, more reduced and blurred with each appearance, until in the distance it becomes no more than a dubious whirl of snow.

And yet it is undoubtedly the same boy who precedes the soldier as he enters the café. Before going in the child shakes his black cape and takes off his beret, hitting it twice on the wooden upright of the glazed door to knock off the bits of ice that have formed inside the folds. The soldier must have met him several times therefore, as he walked round and round within the criss-cross of identical streets. He never, in any case, came to any boulevard, any road that was wider or planted with trees or different in any way whatsoever. The child had finally mentioned a few names, the names of the few streets he knew, obviously useless.

He is hitting his beret smartly now against the wooden upright of a glazed door, in front of which they have both stopped. The interior is brightly lit. A short gathered curtain of white, translucent material conceals the view through the lower part of the pane. But from a man's eye-level the whole room can easily be observed: the counter on the left, the tables in the middle, and to the right a wall covered with notices of various sizes. There are few drinkers at this late hour; two workmen sitting at one of the tables and a character, more elaborately dressed, standing by the zinc counter, over which the proprietor is leaning forward. The latter is a man of massive build, made more remarkable still by the slightly elevated position he holds in relation to his customer. They have both turned their heads at the same time towards the glazed door which the boy has just hit with his beret.

But they see only the soldier's face, above the net curtain. And the child, turning the handle of the door with one hand, with the other hits his beret a second time against the upright which is already moving away from the frame. The proprietor's eyes have left the soldier's blanched face, still starkly visible against the blackness of the night and cut off by the curtain at the chin, and lower their gaze along the gap that is widening more and more between the door and its frame to admit the child.

Once inside the child turns and beckons to the soldier to follow him. This time all eyes are fixed on the new arrival: those of the proprietor behind his counter, those of the well-dressed character standing in front of the counter, those of the two workmen sitting at the table. One of them, who had had his back to the door, has pivoted on his chair, without letting go of his half-empty glass of red wine which stands on the chequered oilcloth in the middle of the table. The other glass, just beside the first, is also gripped by a big hand, which wholly conceals the glass's possible contents. To the left a circle of reddish liquid marks another place previously occupied by one of these two glasses, or by a third.

Then it is the soldier himself sitting in front of a similar glass, half-full of the same dark wine. On the red and white chequerboard of the oilcloth the glass has left several circular stains, most of them incomplete, making a series of more or less closed arcs, overlapping each other here and there, nearly dry in some places, still wet and shiny in others, where a film remains on the darker deposit already formed, while in other parts of the network the pattern is more blurred by successive movements of a glass, too close together, or even half-erased by sliding movements, or else, perhaps, by the rapid flick of a rag.

The soldier is still waiting at the foot of his lamp-post, motionless, his two hands in the pockets of his coat, the same parcel under his left arm. It is daylight again, the same dull and pallid daylight. But the street-lamp is extinguished. The same houses, the same deserted streets, the same white and grey colours, the same cold.

The snow has stopped falling. The layer on the ground is hardly any thicker, just a little more piled up perhaps. And the yellowish paths, trodden all along the pavements by hurrying pedestrians, are the same. Apart from those narrow passages the white surface remains unblemished almost everywhere; but some slight changes have nevertheless occurred here and there, such as the circular area trampled by the soldier's big boots, by the lamp-post.

It is the child this time who comes to meet him. At first he is only a vague silhouette, an irregular black smudge approaching quite fast along the outer edge of the pavement. Every time the smudge reaches a lamp-post, it makes a rapid movement towards it and then quickly resumes its forward course in the original direction. It is soon easy to distinguish the narrow black trousers that cling to the nimble legs, the black cape thrown back and flying around the shoulders, the cloth beret pulled right down to the eyes. Every time the child reaches a lamp-post he suddenly stretches out his arm towards the cast-iron column and, gripping it with his woollen-gloved hand, swings his whole body, launched by his running speed, right round this axis, his feet hardly touching the ground, until almost at once he is back in his original position on the outer edge of the pavement, where he resumes his forward course towards the soldier.

He may not immediately have noticed the soldier, who partly merges perhaps with the cast-iron column against which his hip and right arm are resting. But in order better to observe the boy and his progress, cut by loops with accompanying whirls that each time send the cape flying out, the man has stepped forward a little, and the child, now half-way between the last two lamp-posts, stops abruptly, feet together, hands gathering the hanging flaps of the cape around his stiffened body, his attentive face with its wide-open eyes turned towards the soldier.

'Hello,' says the soldier.

The child considers him without surprise, but also without the slightest sign of good-will, as if he found this further meeting both natural and a bore.

'Where did you sleep?' he says at last.

The soldier makes a vague sign with his chin, not bothering to take his hand out of his pocket:

'Over there.'

'At the barracks?'

'Yes, if you like, at the barracks.'

The child examines the soldier's clothing from head to foot. The greenish army-coat is neither more nor less crumpled, the puttees have been wound as carelessly, the boots have more or less the same splashes of mud on them. But the beard is perhaps blacker still.

'Where is it, your barracks?'

'Over there,' says the soldier.

And he repeats the same sign with his chin, pointing it vaguely behind him, or at his right shoulder.

'You don't know how to wind your puttees,' the child says.

The man lowers his eyes and bends a little forward over his boots.

'Oh, that. It doesn't matter any more now, you know.'

As he straightens up again he notices that the boy is much closer than where he expected to see him: only three or four yards away. He did not think he had stopped so near, nor can he remember having seen him move up since. And yet it would hardly have been possible for the child to have changed his position without the soldier seeing it, just while he had his head lowered: in such a short space of time the child could barely have taken one step. Besides, the attitude he is standing in is exactly the same as at the beginning of the conversation: rigid in the black cape, which he is holding closed—drawn tight in fact around his body—with two invisible hands, his eyes raised.

'Twelve thousand three hundred and forty-five,' says the child, reading the army number on the coat collar.

'Yes,' says the soldier. 'But it isn't my number.'

'It is. It's written on you.'

'Oh, you know, now. . . .'

'It's even written twice.'

And the child sticks out an arm from under his cape and stretches it forward horizontally, pointing his index finger at the two red lozenges. He is wearing a navy blue sweater and a knitted woollen glove of the same colour.

'All right . . . if you like,' says the soldier.

The child returns his arm under the cape, and closes the cape carefully, holding it closed from inside.

'What's in your parcel?'

'I've already told you.'

The child suddenly turns his head towards the door of the building. The soldier, thinking the child has seen something unusual, follows his gaze, but he can see only the same vertical strip of darkness, a hand's width, which separates the hinged leaf of the door, now ajar, from the fixed leaf. As the boy goes on watching it attentively, the man tries to make out some outline in the shadow of the entrance, but without result.

Finally he asks:

'What are you looking at?'

'What's in your parcel?' the child repeats instead of answering, and without taking his eyes off the slightly open door.

'I've already told you—some things.'

'What things?'

'Things of mine.'

The boy turns his gaze back to the soldier:

'You've got a kit-bag to put them in. All soldiers have kit-bags.'

He has become more assured during the dialogue. His voice is now no longer distant but decisive, almost peremptory. The man on the contrary is speaking lower and lower:

'It's over, you know, now. The war's over. . . .'

He is aware again of his fatigue. He no longer feels like answering this interrogation that leads to nothing. He would almost be prepared to hand his parcel over to the boy. He stares at the brown wrapping-paper that covers the box under his arm; the snow on it, in drying, has left some darker rings, rounded outlines laced with minute fringing; the slackened string has slipped towards one of the corners.

Beyond the boy who is still standing motionless the soldier looks at the totally empty street. And turning in the opposite direction he sees once more the same flattened perspective.

'You wouldn't know what time it is?' he says, resuming his original position against the cast-iron column.

The boy shakes his head several times, from left to right and from right to left.

'Your father—does he serve meals, to customers?'

'He's not my father,' says the child.

And before the man can rephrase his question he pivots on his heel and walks mechanically towards the slightly open door. He climbs the step, pushes the leaf a little, slips into the aperture and closes the door behind him, not slamming it but making a clearly audible click as the latch moves into place.

The soldier now has only the snowy pavement to stare at, with its yellowish path on the right and, to the left of that, a virgin surface marked by one solitary regular trail: two small-sized shoes at big-stride intervals along the edge of the pavement, parallel to the gutter, and then, about four yards from the last street-lamp, coming together in a more trampled spot and turning at a right angle, in small steps, to rejoin the path and the narrower passage leading from the path to the door of the building.

The soldier raises his head towards the grey façade and its rows of uniform windows without balconies, each underlined by a white sill, hoping perhaps to see the boy appear somewhere behind a window-pane. But he knows very well that the child in the cape does not live here, since he himself has already accompanied him to his home. Judging by the look of the windows the whole building seems, in any case, to be unoccupied.

The heavy red curtains cover the whole height from floor to ceiling. The wall facing these is furnished with the chest of drawers and, above it, the picture. The child is there in his place, squatting on the floor with his legs folded; looking as if he wanted to creep right under the bench. Yet he continues to observe the foreground of the scene with an attention that can be gauged, if by nothing else, by his wide-open eyes.

This gauge is, it is true, a little uncertain: if the artist considered that the scene opened out on nothing, if in his mind there is nothing on the fourth side of this rectangular room of which he has depicted three walls only, it could be said that the child's eyes are staring at nothing but into space. But in that case it was not logical to choose, for this neutralisation of the child, the only one of the four sides which probably does give on to something. In the three walls represented in the engraving no kind of opening is visible. Even if there is an exit at the back on the left, behind the coat-stands, it is certainly not the main entrance to the café, the interior layout of which would then be too abnormal. The entrance-door, always a glazed door, bearing in white enamel letters stuck on the glass the word 'café' and the name of the proprietor in two curved lines seen on their concave side, then, below, a gathered curtain of some light, translucent material making it necessary for anyone looking in to come right up against the door, such an entrance-door can only be in the drawing's missing wall, the rest of which would consist of a large front-window, also veiled up to half its height and across its width by a long net curtain and decorated in the middle with three balls in low relief—one red above two white—at any rate if the exit behind the coat-stands leads to a billiard-room.

The boy sitting with the box in his arms would then be looking towards the entrance. But he is squatting on the floor and certainly cannot see the street over the top of the curtain. His eyes are not raised to catch sight of some wan face glued to the pane, cut off at the neck by the net curtain. His gaze is more or less horizontal. Could the door have just opened to let in a new arrival who astonishes the boy by his peculiar dress: a soldier, for instance? Such a solution seems doubtful, for the door is more usually situated on the side of the counter, that is in this case on the extreme left, where a small empty space extends in front of the well-dressed characters standing there. The child on the contrary is sitting to the right of the picture where, among the clutter of benches and tables, there is no passage giving access to the rest of the room.

41

Besides, the soldier came in a long time ago: he is sitting at a table a long way behind the child, who seems to take no interest in his uniform. The soldier is also staring straight ahead towards the foreground, and at a barely higher level; but since he is much further away from the front of the café, he only needs to raise his eyes very slightly to see the pane above the curtain, and the snow falling densely, once more erasing the footprints, the trails of solitary footsteps, the yellowish paths running along below the high façades.

Just at the corner of the last house, standing against the quoin, within the L-shaped band of white snow between the wall and the yellowish path, his body vertically cut by the angle of the stone which hides one foot, one leg, one shoulder and a whole panel of the black cape, the boy is watching; his eyes are fixed on the cast-iron lamp-post. Has he re-emerged from the building by another door opening on the transverse street? Or has he climbed out through one of the ground-floor windows? The soldier pretends in any case not to have noticed his reappearance. Leaning against his lamp-post, he is concentrating on the deserted roadway, towards the distant extremity of the street.

'What are you waiting for?' Then in the same tone, like an echo, after some ten seconds: 'What are you waiting there for?'

The voice is indeed that of the boy, a calm, reflective voice, without kindness, a little too deep for a child of ten or twelve. But it seems very close, two or three yards away at most, whereas the corner of the building is at least eight yards away. The man has a strong urge to turn and check the distance, and find out whether the child has once again moved nearer. Or is he, without looking at the child, going to give him any old answer: 'The tram', or 'Supper', to make him understand he is being a nuisance? He continues to inspect his surroundings.

When at last he transfers his gaze towards the boy, the latter has completely vanished. The soldier waits another minute, thinking he has merely stepped back behind the stone quoin and will soon risk a peep from his hiding-place. But nothing of the sort occurs.

The man lowers his eyes to the virgin snow where the footprints of a moment ago turn at right-angles just in front of him. In the part along the pavement edge, the footprints are spaced out and distorted by running, with a small mass of snow piled up behind by the movement of the shoe; the few steps that rejoin the path, on the contrary, show the design of the soles with great precision; a set of chevrons over the whole width of the foot and, in the heel, a cross-shaped hollow inside an embossed circle—that is, on the shoe itself, a cross embossed inside a circular depression cut into the rubber (a second round hole, much shallower and smaller in diameter, being perhaps still there at the centre of the cross, with figures in relief showing the size: one, one an a half perhaps, or two).

The soldier, who had bent forward a little to examine the details of the footprint, now rejoins the trail. Coming to the door of the building, he tries to push it open, but it resists the pressure: it really is shut. The door is made of solid wood, with mouldings, the leaf framed by two very narrow fixed sections. The man walks on towards the corner of the house and turns into the transverse street, which is similarly deserted.

This new road leads, like the previous one, to a right-angled crossroads where the last lamp stands some ten yards before the point where the pavement edge curves round, and all around are identical façades. Around the conical base of this lamp-post too winds a stalk of cast-iron ivy, undulating in the same way, with exactly the same leaves in the same places, the same ramifications, the same accidents of growth, the same faults in the metal. The whole design is emphasised by the same edgings of snow. Perhaps it was at this crossroads that the meeting was to take place.

The soldier lifts his eyes to look for the enamel plaques that should give the names of these streets. On one face the stone quoin bears no indication at all. On the other, about ten feet up, is the regulation blue plaque, with its enamel chipped off in chunks, as if some boys had hurled stones at it, using it as a target; only the word 'Rue' is legible still, and further on the two letters 'na' followed by a down-stroke broken by the concentric cracks of the next hole. The name must have been very short. The damage is fairly old, for the exposed metal is already deeply gnawed with rust.

Just as he is about to cross the street, still following the narrow yellowed path, to see if he cannot find some other plaques in better condition, he hears a voice quite close speaking three or four syllables whose meaning he has not time to catch. He turns at once; but there is no one around. No doubt, in this solitude, the snow carries sound in an odd way.

The voice was deep and yet was not like a man's voice. . . . A young woman with a very deep voice perhaps; there are some. But the memory of it is too fugitive: already only a neutral tone remains, characterless, which might belong to anyone, even leaving some doubt as to whether it was a human voice. At this moment the soldier notices that the door of the corner building is not shut. He takes a few steps forward, mechanically, in that direction. It is impossible to make out anything through the gap, the interior is so dark. All the windows, to the right, to the left, up above, are closed; the black panes, dirty, uncurtained, showing no sign of life in the unlighted rooms, as if the entire building were abandoned.

The door is made of solid wood, with mouldings, and is painted dark brown. The slightly open leaf is

45

framed by two much narrower, fixed sections; the
soldier pushes it further. When the door is wide
open he climbs the snow-covered step, already
marked by many feet, and crosses the threshold.

He is standing at one end of a dark corridor with
several doors. At the other end he can just make out
the beginning of a staircase, rising out of the continuation of the corridor and vanishing into the
darkness. The far end of this long and narrow
entrance also gives access to another, perpendicular
corridor, indicated only by a thickening of the
darkness, just before the staircase, running off on
either side. All this is empty, denuded of those
domestic objects that are the usual signs of life in a
house: doormats, a pram left at the bottom of the
stairs, a bucket and broom leaning in a corner.
Here there is nothing but the floor and walls; and
the walls are bare, painted all over a very dark
colour; on the left, just by the entrance, the small
white notice about passive resistance and what to
do in case of fire, can be made out. The floor is of
plain wood, blackened by mud and clumsy scrub-
bing, as are the first few steps of the stairs, the only
ones visible. After five or six steps the staircase
seems to turn towards the right. The soldier can
now see the wall at the other end. And there,
squeezing herself as much as she can into the corner,
her two arms stiff beside her body which she is
pressing against the wall, a woman in a full skirt
and a long apron tied tightly round her waist is

46

looking towards the open door of the house and the silhouette revealed against the light.

Before the man has a chance to say a word a side door suddenly opens on the left of the corridor and another aproned woman, more ample than the first, perhaps older as well, takes a step forward. She looks up, stops, opens her mouth to an immoderate width and, retreating step by step into her own doorway, starts shrieking loudly, the sound rising higher and higher in pitch until it ends abruptly with the violent slamming of the door. At the same moment footsteps rush loudly up the wooden stairs; it is the other woman running away, towards the higher floors, disappearing too, in a split second, although the hammering of her clogs continues up, the pace not slowing, the noise however decreasing progressively with each floor as the young woman hurries on, her full skirt beating round her legs, half held with one hand perhaps, the sound marking not the slightest halt for breath at any of the landings, which are merely suggested by the different resonance at the beginning and end of each flight: one floor, two floors, three or four floors, or even more.

Then complete silence again. But another door, this time on the right of the corridor, has opened slightly. Or was it already open just now? More probably the sudden uproar has attracted this new figure, again rather similar to the first two, or to the first one at least: a woman, also young-looking,

47

in a long, dark grey apron tied tightly round her waist and puffed out over the hips. Her eyes now meet the soldier's, and she asks:

'What is it?'

Her voice is deep, low, but without expression, and this with a premeditated air as if she wished to remain as impersonal as possible. It could also have been the voice heard from the street a moment ago.

'They're afraid,' says the soldier.

'Yes,' the woman says. 'It's seeing you like that. . . . And with the light behind you . . . It's hard to see . . . They took you for a . . .'

She does not finish the sentence. She is standing quite still, scrutinising him. Nor does she open her door any further, no doubt feeling more secure inside, holding on to the jamb with one hand and the door with the other, ready to shut it. She asks:

'What do you want?'

'I'm looking for a street . . .' the soldier says, 'a street I had to go to.'

'What street?'

'That's the trouble. I can't remember the name. Something like Galabier, or Matadier. But I'm not sure. More like Montoret, perhaps?'

The woman seems to be thinking.

'It's big, you know, the town,' she says at last.

'But it's somewhere round here, according to the directions I was given.'

The young woman turns her head towards the

48

interior of the flat and, in a louder voice, asks somebody off-stage: 'D'you know a rue Montaret? Near here. Or something that sounds like that?'

She waits, her regular profile visible in the opening of the door. All is dark behind her: it must be a hall with no windows. The fat woman too came out of total darkness. After a moment a distant voice replies in a few mumbled words and the woman turns her face back towards the soldier:

'Wait a minute, I'll go and see.'

She starts pushing the door to, then stops:

'Close the street-door,' she says. 'It makes the whole house cold.'

The soldier walks back to the door and pushes the leaf shut with a slight click: the latch slipping into place. Now he is in the dark again. The woman's door must also be closed. It is impossible for him to make his way towards her for there is nothing to orientate him, not a single gleam. It is total night. No sound is to be heard either: no steps, no stifled whispers, no clinking of kitchenware. The whole house seems uninhabited. The soldier shuts his eyes and sees again the white flakes slowly falling, the line of street-lamps punctuating his path from end to end of the snow-covered pavement, and the boy running off at full speed, appearing and disappearing, visible for a few seconds at a time in each succeeding patch of light, getting smaller and smaller, at intervals equal in time but with the spaces made shorter and shorter by the distance, so that he seems to be moving more and more slowly as he diminishes in size

From the chest of drawers to the table is six steps: three to the fireplace and three more after that. It is five steps from the table to the corner of the bed; four steps from the bed to the chest of drawers. The path from the chest of drawers to the table is not quite straight: it curves gently to pass nearer the fireplace. Above the mantelpiece there is a mirror, a large, rectangular mirror, hanging on the wall. The foot of the bed is exactly opposite.

Suddenly the light comes on again in the corridor. It is no longer the same light and it does not directly illuminate the place where the soldier stands, which remains in shadow. It is at the other end of the corridor, an artificial light, yellow and pale, coming from the section of the transverse corridor that goes off to the right. A luminous rectangle is thus thrown on to the end wall on the right, just before the stairs, and a lighted area splays out from there, drawing two slanting lines on the floor: one crossing the blackened floorboards of the corridor, the other sloping up the first three steps: beyond that line, and this side of the other, darkness remains, though slightly attenuated.

Still on that side, in the invisible area where the light is coming from, a door shuts softly and a key turns in a lock. Then the light goes out. And once again all is in darkness. But footsteps, probably guided by old familiarity with the place, are moving along the transverse passage. It is a pliant step, not heavy, yet definite, unhesitating. Now it is at the foot of the stairs right opposite the soldier, who, to avoid the collision of two bodies in the dark, stretches out his hands like a blind man around him, seeking a wall against which he can flatten himself. But the steps do not come in his direction: instead of turning into the corridor at the end of which he is standing they go straight on into the left-hand section of the transverse corridor. A latch is turned and a cruder light, the light from outside, invades this left-hand part of the corridor, increasing in intensity to a dull grey semi-daylight. There must therefore be a second door on to the street. That would be the door through which the boy re-emerged. Soon the light disappears, just as it came, gradually, and the door shuts, bringing a return of total obscurity.

Darkness. Click. Yellow light. Click. Darkness. Click. Grey light. Click. Darkness. And the footsteps sounding on the wooden floor of the corridor. And the footsteps sounding on the asphalt, in the street that is stiff with frost. And the snow beginning to fall. And the boy's recurring silhouette diminishing in size from lamp-post to lamp-post.

If that last person had gone out not by the same door as the boy but on this side of the building, he or she would, in opening the door, have let in the light on to this part of the corridor and so have discovered the soldier pressed flat against the wall, suddenly illuminated, only a few inches away. As in the case of a collision in the dark, new shrieks might then have stirred up the whole house again, making shadows scamper towards the staircase, causing terrified faces to peer out of doorways, neck tense, eyes anxious, mouth already opening to yell. . . .

'There's no rue Montalet, not round here, or anything like it,' the deep voice announces; and then at once: 'What—are you in the dark? You should have switched the light on.' At these words the light returns to the corridor, a yellow light that falls from a naked bulb on the end of a flex, illuminating the young woman in the grey apron whose arm is still stretched out from the doorway; the hand resting on the white porcelain switch falls away as the light eyes stare at the man, moving down from the hollow cheeks with the beard now almost a quarter of an inch thick, to the box wrapped in brown paper and on down to the clumsily wound puttees, then back up to the drawn features of the face.

'You are tired,' she says.

It is not a question. The voice is again neutral, low, without intonation, mistrustful perhaps. The soldier makes a vague gesture with his free hand; a half smile draws up one corner of his mouth.

'You're not wounded, are you?'

The free hand rises a little higher. 'No, no,' says the man, 'I'm not wounded.'

And the hand moves slowly down again. Then they stand there for a while, looking at each other in silence.

'What are you going to do,' the woman asks at last, 'when you've lost the name of the street?'

'I don't know,' says the soldier.

'Was it important?'

'Yes . . . No . . . Probably.'

After another silence the young woman asks:

'What was it?'

'I don't know,' says the soldier.

He is tired, he wants to sit down, anywhere, there against the wall. He repeats mechanically:

'I don't know.'

'You don't know what you were going there for?'

'I had to go there to find out.'

'Ah!'

'I had to meet someone. It'll be too late now.'

During this dialogue the woman has opened her door wide and has stepped forward into the opening. She is wearing a black dress with a long full skirt, which is three-quarters covered by a grey apron gathered at the waist and knotted round the back. The lower half of the apron is very full, like the skirt, whereas the top half is only a simple square of cloth protecting the front of the dress. Her face has regular and very sharp features. Her hair is black. But the eyes are light in colour, a sort of

53

blue-green or grey-blue. They do not try and avoid his; on the contrary they rest for a long time on the man, though without betraying any expression whatsoever.

'You haven't eaten,' she says. And this time a fleeting hint of pity, perhaps, or fear, or astonishment, wavers in the sentence.

But as soon as the sentence is finished and the silence has returned it becomes impossible to recapture the intonation which seemed just now to have some meaning—fear, boredom, doubt, solicitude, some interest or other—and only the statement remains: 'You haven't eaten,' uttered in a neutral tone. The man repeats his evasive gesture.

'Come in a moment,' she says, perhaps regretfully —or perhaps not.

Click. Darkness. Click. Yellow light now illuminating a small entrance hall with just room for a circular coat-stand, loaded with hats and clothes. Click. Darkness.

A door now opens into a square room, furnished with a divan, a rectangular table and a marble-topped chest of drawers. The table is covered with a red and white chequered oilcloth. A fireplace, with the shutter raised on a hearth with no firedogs, only cold ashes, occupies the centre of one wall. To the right of the fireplace is another door, which is ajar, leading to a very dark room or a box-cupboard.

'Here,' says the young woman, pointing to a straw-bottomed chair drawn up to the table. 'Sit down.' The soldier pulls the chair out a little, holding it by the top of the back, and sits down. He rests his right hand and his elbow on the oilcloth. His left hand remains in his coat pocket, the box wrapped in brown paper still held tight between his arm and his body.

In the opening of the door, but a step or two beyond it, very indistinct in the darkness, the silhouette of a child stands motionless, turned towards the man in army uniform whom his mother (is it his mother?) has just shown into the flat, and who is sitting at the table, at a slight angle to it, half leaning on the red oilcloth, shoulders hunched and head bent forward.

The woman makes her re-entry, through the door leading from the hall. In one hand, held against her hip, she is carrying a piece of bread and a glass; the other arm hangs down her body, the hand gripping a bottle by the neck. She places everything on the table, in front of the soldier.

Without speaking she fills the glass to the brim. Then she leaves the room again. It is an ordinary litre-bottle made of colourless glass, half-full of a dark red wine; the glass, standing in front of it, just by the man's hand, is crudely made, shaped like a cylindrical mug and fluted on the lower half. The bread is on the left: the end of a big brown loaf, which in section is a semi-circle with rounded corners; its texture is tight-grained, with minute regular holes. The man's hand is red, roughened by hard work and the cold; the fingers, folded back into the palm, are covered with innumerable little crevices around the knuckles; they are moreover stained with black, as if by grease adhering to the creviced areas of the skin, which a perfunctory wash had not removed. Thus the bony protuberance at the base of the index-finger is hatched with short black lines, most of them parallel to each other, or slightly divergent, others lying quite differently, surrounding the first or cutting across them.

Above the chimney, a large rectangular mirror hangs on the wall; the wall it reflects is that of which the lower part is occupied by the large chest of drawers. Right in the centre of the wall is a full-length photograph of a soldier in battledress—perhaps the husband of the young woman with the deep voice and the light eyes, and perhaps the father of the child. A coat with the flaps folded back, puttees, heavy marching boots: the uniform is that of the infantry, as witness also the helmet with chin-strap and the complete gear of packs, kit-bag, flask, belt, cartridge-cases, etc. The man is gripping with both hands, just above his belt, the two straps that cross over his chest; he wears a carefully trimmed moustache; the total effect is neat and, as it were, lacquered, due no doubt to skilful touching-up by the specialist who made the enlargement; the face itself, graced with a conventional smile, has been so scraped, changed, softened, that now it has no character left, and resembles for ever all those pictures of soldiers about to leave for the front or sailors about to sail that are displayed in every photographer's window. And yet the original snap-shot seems to have been taken by an amateur—the young woman, probably, or a friend from his regi-ment—for the background is not that of a fake middle-class drawing-room, or a pseudo-verandah with trees and a park painted on a *trompe-l'oeil* backcloth, but the street just outside the door of the building, near the gaslamp with the conical base round which is twined a garland of stylised ivy.

The man's equipment is brand new. The photo-graph must date from the beginning of the war, the time of the general mobilisation or the first call-up of reservists, or from an even earlier date: during military service or a brief period of training. Yet the soldier's full battledress would rather seem to indicate that this was actually at the beginning of the war, for an infantryman on leave does not come home so cumbersomely attired in normal times. The most likely occasion would therefore have been a very special leave of a few hours, granted to the mobilised for family farewells, just before leaving for the front. No friend from his regiment was with him, for then the young woman would also have appeared in the snapshot, beside the soldier; it must have been her that took the photograph, with her own camera; no doubt she even devoted a whole film to the occasion, and later chose the best picture for enlargement.

57

The man has gone out in the sun because there is not enough light inside the flat; he has simply walked out of the door, and has found it natural to stand by the lamp-post. So that the light shall fall on his face, he is looking up the street, with the stone quoin of the building behind him on the right (that is to say, on his left); the lamp-post stands on the other side, the hem of the coat just touching it. The soldier glances down and for the first time notices the ivy branch moulded in the cast-iron. The palmate leaves with five pointed lobes, each with its five raised veins, are borne on a fairly long peduncle; at the junction of each leaf the stem changes direction, but the alternate curves thus formed are rather slight on one side and on the contrary very marked on the other, so that the general effect is of a downward curve, preventing the branch from climbing to to any height and allowing it to twine round the cone; then it divides in two and the the upper, shorter branch, bearing only three leaves (the last one very small), rises in an attenuated sinusoid; the other branch vanishes towards the other side of the cone and the edge of the pavement. As soon as the roll of film is finished, the soldier goes back into the building.

The corridor is dark, as usual. The door of the flat has remained ajar; he pushes it, crosses the unlighted hall and goes in to sit at the table, where his wife serves him some wine. He drinks, without saying anything, in small sips, each time replacing his glass on the chequered oilcloth. When this performance has been repeated a number of times the surrounding space is almost completely covered with circular stains, most of them incomplete, making a series of more or less closed arcs, overlapping each other here and there, nearly dry in some places, in others still gleaming with fresh liquid. Between mouthfuls of wine the soldier keeps his eyes lowered on this disorderly network which becomes more complex every minute. He does not know what to say. He ought to go now. But when he has finished his glass the woman pours him another; and he drinks that too, in small sips, and slowly eats the rest of the bread. The silhouette of the child, which he had noticed through the partly-open door of the next room, has dissolved into the darkness.

When the soldier makes up his mind to raise his eyes and look at the young woman she is sitting facing him: not at the table but on a chair placed (has she put it there?) in front of the chest of drawers, under the black frame of the portrait hanging on the wall. She is gazing at her visitor's crumpled and soiled uniform; her grey eyes move up towards the collar where the two pieces of red felt are sewn, bearing the army number.

'What regiment is it?' she says at last, with a forward movement of her face to indicate the two light red lozenges.

'I don't know,' says the soldier.

This time the woman shows some astonishment: 'You've forgotten that too—the name of your own regiment?'

'No, it's not that. . . . But this isn't my coat.'

The young woman sits still for a moment saying nothing. And yet a question seems to be hovering in her mind, a question she cannot quite formulate, or which she hesitates to put directly. And indeed, after a whole minute of silence, or even more, she asks:

'And whom did it belong to?'

'I don't know,' says the soldier.

Besides, if he had known, he would probably also have been able to tell what regiment the light red lozenges represented. He looks again at the enlarged photograph on the wall above the woman's black hair. The picture is oval in shape, fading out at the edges; the paper all around it has remained a creamy-white, right up to the rectangular frame of very dark wood. At this distance the distinguishing marks on the coat collar are not visible. The uniform, in any case, is that of the infantry. The man must have been stationed in the town itself, or in the neighbourhood, while waiting to leave for the front line; otherwise he could not have come to kiss his wife good-bye. But where are the barracks in this town? Are there several? What units would be seen here in ordinary times?

The soldier thinks he should take an interest in these things: they would provide a harmless, normal subject of conversation. But he has hardly opened his mouth when he notices a change in his interlocutor's attitude. She is looking at him through slightly narrowed eyes, as if watching for his next words with an attentiveness that is exaggeratedly sharp, considering the little importance he attaches to them himself. He stops at once, on an uncertain phrase that swerves hastily in a direction unheralded by its beginning, and so vaguely interrogative that the woman can reserve the right to abstain from answering. This is in fact the solution she adopts. But her features remain contracted. These questions are indeed the very ones that a clumsy spy might ask; and mistrust is natural in such circumstances. . . . Although it is now a little late for concealing the disposition of military objectives from the enemy.

The soldier has finished his bread and wine. He has no further reason for remaining in this house, in spite of his desire to enjoy for a moment longer the relative warmth, the uncomfortable chair and the wary presence of the woman facing him. He ought to find a way of taking his leave gracefully, so as to mitigate the impression left by the recent misunderstanding. To try and justify himself would certainly make things worse; and how would he convincingly explain his ignorance about . . . The soldier now tries to recall the exact terms he has just used. There was the word 'barracks', but he cannot manage to recall the strange phrase he uttered; he is not even certain of having actually mentioned the whereabouts of the buildings, and even less of having unambiguously shown that he did not know where they were.

Without noticing it he has perhaps passed a barracks during his wanderings. And yet he cannot remember any construction in the traditional style: a low building (two floors only of identical windows framed in red brick) some hundred yards long, with a low-pitched slate roof topped by big rectangular chimneys also made of brick. The whole thing stands behind a vast, bare, gravelled courtyard that is separated from the boulevard and its densely foliaged trees by very high metal railings, buttressed and bristling with sharp points both inside and out. Here and there a sentry-box shelters an armed guard standing at ease; the boxes are made of wood with zinc roofs, and large black and red chevrons painted on both sides.

The soldier has seen nothing like that. He has walked along no railings; he has noticed no vast gravelled courtyard; he has encountered neither thick foliage nor sentry-boxes, nor of course has he seen any armed guards standing at ease. He has not even come across a single boulevard planted with trees. He has only wandered through the same rectilinear streets, between two high rows of flat façades; but a barracks could also look like that. The sentry-boxes have naturally been removed, like everything that could distinguish the building from those on either side of it; only the metal bars are left, protecting the ground-floor windows almost up to their full height. They consist of vertical rods, square in section, a hand's width apart, joined by two transverse bars, one near the top and one near the bottom. The upper part is free, ending in points some seven or eight inches below the top of the window; the lower ends of the bars must be bedded into the stone of the window-sill, but this detail is not visible on account of the snow that has accumulated there, forming an irregular layer over the whole horizontal surface, very thick particularly on the right-hand side.

But, for that matter, this could just as well be a fire-station or a convent or a school or offices, or merely a house with its ground-floor windows protected by railings. As he reaches the next crossroads the soldier turns at right-angles into the adjoining street.

And the snow goes on falling, slow, vertical, uniform, and the white layer thickens imperceptibly on the projecting parts of the window-sills, on the doorsteps, on the raised parts of the black lamp-posts, on the street without traffic, on the deserted pavements where already the paths made by the trampling of feet during the day have vanished. And again night is falling.

The even flakes, of constant size, equally

spaced one from the other, all fall at the same speed, keeping the same distances between them and the same disposition, as if they belonged to a single rigid system descending in one continuous movement, vertical, uniform and slow.

The footprints of the late passer-by who is walking past the houses with head bent, from one end of the rectilinear street to the other, appear one by one in the even surface of the snow, now intact again, and into which they already sink half an inch at least. And behind him the snow at once begins to cover the hobnailed pattern of the soles, slowly reconstituting the original whiteness of the crunched-out shape, restoring its grained, velvety, fragile surface, fading out the sharp edges, blurring the outline more and more and finally filling in the whole depression so that there is no perceptible difference in level with the surrounding areas, and the continuity is re-established, and the whole surface is even again, intact and unimpaired.

And so the soldier cannot know if anyone else has passed there, along the houses with their unlighted windows, some time before. And when he reaches the next crossroads the transverse street is likewise devoid of furrowed trails, nor does this signify anything either.

Yet the boy's footprints are slower to disappear. For he leaves a trail of little heaps behind him as he runs: the sole of each shoe, in springing up violently, flings back a little pile of snow which then remains at the instep of the foot (where the shape is at its narrowest) in a smaller or larger mound which necessarily takes longer than the rest to efface; and the holes made on either side, by the toe and the heel, are all the deeper in that the boy does not follow the day's old paths but prefers to go along the edge where the snow is thicker (though the eye can detect no difference) and where the steps sink deeper. Moreover, since he is advancing very fast the length of his trail, from the spot where he is now to the last disturbance still discernible under the fresh layer, the length of his trail is much greater than that of the soldier's, especially with the loops that punctuate the child's trail, around each lamp-post.

These loops, it is true, are not unmistakably in evidence, for the boy hardly touches the ground with his feet as he swings round the lamp-post, gripping the cast-iron column. As for the design of the rubber soles, that is already blurred: neither the little chevrons nor the cross in the centre of its circle are identifiable, even before the falling snow has begun to cover up the pattern. In fact, what with the distortions arising out of the running motion, and the uncertainty as to the details of his course, there is really nothing to differentiate this trail from any other left by a child of the same age—who might, after all, be wearing shoes with identical soles (the same shoes, perhaps, from the same shop) and swing round the lamp-posts in a similar way.

There are, in any case, no marks of any kind in the snow, no trace of footprints, and the snow goes on falling on the deserted street, uniform, vertical and slow. The night must be completely dark now and the flakes are only visible as they pass through the light of a lamp. And so the street is punctuated at constant intervals (which however seem shorter and shorter the further away they are, both to the right and to the left), punctuated with lighter zones where the darkness is stippled with innumerable minute white spots, linked in a common falling motion. The window being on the top floor, all these circles of light must seem very pale and distant, at the bottom of the long trench formed by the two parallel rows of houses; so distant even, so tremulous, that it is of course impossible to pick out the flakes one from the other : seen from so high up, they merely form a vague, whitish halo here and there, itself quite blurred because the street-lamps emit only the feeblest glow, made more uncertain still by the dull light given off by all these pale surfaces, the ground, the sky, the curtain of massed flakes falling slowly but steadily past the windows, so thick that it now wholly masks the opposite building, the cast-iron lamp-posts, the last late passer-by, the entire street.

Perhaps the street-lamps have not even been lit this evening, tonight, that night. As for the sound of steps, muffled by the fresh snow, it could not penetrate to such a height from so far away, through the metal shutters, the glass panes, the thick velvet curtains.

The shadow of the fly on the ceiling has stopped just near the spot where the circle of light from the lamp meets the top of the red curtain. Now that it is still its shape becomes more complex: it is indeed an enlargement of the bent filament of the electric bulb, but the main image is repeated not far away by two other identical images, paler, softer, framing the first. Perhaps other images, even less clear, are further multiplied on either side of these; but invisibly, because the whole frail pattern which the fly projects is not in the most brightly lit area of the ceiling but in a fringe of half-light, about an inch wide, that edges the entire periphery of the circle, where the shadow begins.

All the rest of the room, in which only this one lamp standing on the corner of the desk-table is alight, seems relatively dark compared to the glaring circle of light thrown on the white ceiling. The eye that has stared at it too long cannot, when it turns away, see any details on the room's other surfaces. The picture hanging on the far wall is now no more than a grey rectangle framed in black; the chest of drawers below it is merely a dark square with no more volume than the picture, stuck there like a piece of wallpaper; likewise the fireplace in the centre of the perpendicular wall. As for the wall-paper itself, the innumerable, minute spots that make up the pattern no longer have the shape either of flame or flower, or human silhouette, dagger, gas-jet, or in fact of anything at all. They look only like silent feathers falling vertically in regular lines with a steady movement so slow it is hardly perceptible; in fact one would hesitate even to guess its actual direction, whether it is upward or downward, as one would with particles suspended in still water, small bubbles in a gaseous liquid, snowflakes, dust. And on the floor, also in shadow, the gleaming paths have disappeared.

Only the table-top, under the conical lampshade, is lit up, and the bayonet lying in the centre of it. The short stout blade, symmetrically double-edged, is composed of two complimentary sloping polished-steel surfaces, one on either side of the median axis, one of which reflects the light of the lamp's rays into the middle of the room.

On the other side, in the centre of the wall, the picture is so obscured by the darkness that it is hardly more than a grey oval inside a white rectangle, set vertically, and itself framed in black.

At this moment a hesitant voice is heard, fairly near, indistinct. The soldier lowers his eyes from the picture of the soldier on the wall to the young woman sitting on the chair in front of the chest of drawers. But the voice just heard was not hers; as deep perhaps, and not so young, it was certainly a man's voice this time. And anyway it repeats a sentence containing approximately the same sounds, and as incomprehensible, while the young woman

68

remains with her lips closed, sitting straight on the chair, her eyes turned towards the corner of the room where the door is ajar, on the other side of the table. Nothing can be seen in the black gap between the frame and the open edge of the door that leads into the next room.

The young woman is now standing in front of this door, which she pushes further open, just enough to slip through; then the door moves back, without shutting completely, leaving the same gap as before. And in the black space of this gap the child now reappears.

Or at any rate a vertical strip of him reappears, including one eye, the nose, three-quarters of the mouth and chin, a long rectangle of blue smock, half a naked knee, a sock, a black felt slipper, the whole quite rigid as the man's voice repeats the same sentence for the third time, but with less force so that again no words can be recognised, only outlines of sounds devoid of meaning. The woman's deep voice replies, lower still, almost a murmur. The child's eye just reaches the level of the door-knob, which is made of white porcelain and is ovoid in shape. On the other side the electric switch, also of porcelain, is fixed quite near the door-frame. An argument has begun; the young woman is doing most of the talking, speaking quickly, giving long explanations in which the same groups of words seem to recur with identical intonations. The man's voice only intervenes with short phrases, monosyllables, and even grunts. The child, becoming bolder, opens the door a little wider.

No, it is not the child, for on the contrary he disappears and is replaced by the young woman, whose head appears a little higher in the widened gap.

'It wasn't Boulard, was it?'

And as the soldier stares at her questioningly she repeats: 'Rue Boulard. Was that what you were looking for?'

'No . . . I don't think so . . .' says the soldier indecisively. Then after a moment's reflection and with a little more assurance he shakes his head several times from right to left: 'I don't think so. No.' But the woman has already gone and the door is now shut right to.

The shiny white oval of the door-knob has several points of light on it; the brightest at first glance is near the top: a second one, much larger but less bright, forms a sort of four-sided curved polygon to the right. Lines of light, too, varying in length, width and intensity, follow at various distances the general outline of the convex shape, just as they would on a drawing of it to simulate the relief.

But these concentric lines, instead of giving the object a third dimension, seem rather to make it turn upon itself: staring at it insistently the soldier can see the porcelain knob moving, hardly perceptibly at first, and then increasingly, the long axis of the oval turning through some ten to twenty degrees alternately on either side of the vertical. Nevertheless the door does not open. But perhaps the child, behind it, is playing with the handle, with the other white porcelain door-knob, identical to this one and symmetrically placed in a corresponding position on the other side of the door.

When the door opens, it admits neither the timid, curious child nor the young woman with light eyes but a new character altogether: probably the one who was speaking just now in the adjoining room; and it is, in fact, a voice of similar pitch and tone that tells the soldier categorically that there is no rue Boucharet, neither in this district nor in the whole town. The name he was told can only have been 'Boulard'; and the man offers to explain where that street is. 'And it's quite a walk!' he adds, examining the soldier sitting on his chair with his back a little hunched, his hands flat on his thighs, still holding the battered parcel tightly under his arm; the man examines him so intently he seems to be estimating the number of miles the soldier is still capable of covering before collapsing altogether.

The man is himself certainly of call-up age; but he is disabled, which accounts for his civilian status. His left leg appears to be useless; he walks with the help of a wooden crutch under his armpit which he uses with skill, judging by the rapidity with which he has just passed through the door and reached the end of the table, on the edge of which he is now leaning, with his right hand on the red and white chequered oilcloth. Perhaps he is a war casualty: wounded at

71

the beginning of the fighting, maybe, and sent back
home, put on his feet again somehow or other, before
the retreat of the routed armies and the withdrawal
of the military hospitals. He has a thin, well-trimmed
moustache, like the soldier in the photograph. The
resemblance between them is in fact fairly marked,
in so far as any picture of that kind, after so many
scrapings and retouchings, can look like its model.
But, for that very reason, such a picture proves
nothing. The soldier shakes his head several times
to express his disagreement:

'No,' he answers. 'It didn't sound like Bou-
chard . . .'

'Bouvard,' I said.

'I don't think so. No. It was something else.'

'There isn't anything else.'

'And then it was somewhere around here.'

'You know the town, then?'

'No . . . But it's . . .'

'Well, if you don't know how can you tell? I
know this town, I do! I haven't always had this
gammy leg. . . .' With a movement of his chin he
indicates the crutch. 'Your rue Bouvard's right at the
other end!'

The soldier wants to explain that he has good
reason to believe the opposite, or more precisely, to
think that the street he is looking for is not that one.
But it is difficult, without launching upon complicated details, to convince the disabled man, who
seems for his part so sure of himself. Besides, on re-

flection, even the reasons themselves already seem less persuasive. He is about to resign himself to listening to the directions the other man is so insistent about giving him when the young woman comes back into the room through the door which has been left open. She seems displeased. She takes quick steps as if she has been delayed by some sudden urgent task that prevented her from coming in with the man a few moments before, or even from keeping him out of the visitor's sight.

The disabled man has already launched upon his topographical explanation, filled with a quantity of street-names: Vanizier, Vantardier, Bazaman, Davidson, Tamani, Duroussel, Dirbonne, etc. The young woman interrupts him in mid-itinerary:

'But he said it wasn't Brulard.'

'Not Brulard: Bouvard! I know that street well.' And, turning towards the soldier, as if the answer could never be in doubt: 'It's the depot you're looking for, isn't it?'

'The depot?'

'Yes—the army depot, the one they've been using as auxiliary barracks recently.'

'No,' says the soldier. 'It's not the barracks I'm looking for, or a depot.'

'Well, barracks or no barracks, it makes no difference to where the street is.' Then, suddenly inspired, he drums his fingers on the table and addresses the woman: 'Hey, the boy can take him there, that'll be the simplest thing.'

73

Without altering her dead-pan expression she shrugs her shoulders and replies: 'You know very well I won't have him going out.'

Another discussion starts up between them; another, that is, if the man on the previous occasion was the same as this one. Anyway, in contrast to the dialogue that unfolded then in the adjacent room, it is now mostly the man who speaks, demanding exact reasons for keeping the child shut in, hardly listening to the answers, dogmatically repeating that nobody runs the slightest risk crossing the town, least of all a child, that in any case it won't take him long, it won't even be dark when he returns. The woman counters him with brief, obstinate, irritated phrases:

'You said it was a long way.'

'Only for someone who doesn't know. But not for the boy. He'll go straight there by the shortest route, taking no wrong turns and coming back at once.'

'I'd rather he didn't go out,' the young woman says.

This time the man appeals to the visitor: what possible danger could there be in going out today? Aren't the streets completely quiet? Is anything likely to happen before nightfall? . . . etc.

The soldier says he has no idea. As for the quietness of the streets, that is certainly, for the time being, beyond question.

'But they may arrive at any moment,' the woman says.

The disabled man disagrees: 'Not before to-

74

morrow night,' he asserts, 'or even the day after. Otherwise d'you think he'd be sitting there calmly waiting for them?' He is speaking of the soldier, making a wide, vague gesture over the table in his direction; the soldier for his part does not find this proof very convincing, since he should not be there in any case. But now that the man has again used him in evidence he can only move his hand, barely lifting it from his knee, in a gesture of vague expectancy.

'I don't know,' he says.

He has, moreover, no desire to be led to the other end of the town, although in truth he no longer knows what else he can do. This halt, far from resting him, has filled him with an even greater lassitude. He looks at the young woman with the light eyes, the dead-pan expression, the black hair, the full apron tied tightly round her waist; he looks at the disabled man, whose infirmity does not seem to tire him since he goes on standing there, supported by his crutch, when there is an empty chair just by him. The soldier wonders whether the useless foot is resting on the floor or not, but he cannot tell because the man leaning against the other end of the table is visible only from the top of his thighs: it would therefore be necessary to lean forward, lift the flap of the oilcloth and glance under the table, between the four square legs that taper towards the bottom— or else, tapered towards the bottom, but of turned and fluted wood that, at the top end, becomes cylindrical and smooth, each leg being crowned with

75

a cube bearing a sculptured rose on two of its faces—
or else . . . ; the soldier looks again at the portrait
on the far wall: from this distance the features are
utterly indistinguishable; as for the details of the uniform, they could only be made out if one were
already familiar with them: the two straps crossing
over the chest, the bayonet in its black leather sheath
fixed to the belt, the flaps of the coat folded back, the
puttees . . . unless here it is a question of leggings,
or even boots. . . .

But now the child makes his entry to the left of
the chest of drawers, through the door that leads in
from the hall. He is being pushed forward towards
the soldier who is still sitting at the table. It is the
disabled man who is pushing him from behind with
his free hand, as the crutch makes rapid little movements almost on the same spot, for the boy is not in
fact advancing. The wounded leg is slightly shorter
than the other, or slightly bent, so that the foot moves
an inch or so above the floor.

The child has changed his clothes, probably for
going out: he is now wearing long, narrow trousers
over ankle boots and a thick-knit roll-neck sweater
reaching to his hips; a cape, worn open, hangs from
his shoulders to his knees; his head is covered with a
beret drawn right down on each side over his ears.
The whole outfit is of the same navy-blue colour, or
more precisely of various shades within the navy-
blue range.

The disabled man pushes the child a bit more

firmly from behind so that he now takes a step forward towards the soldier; at the same time he brings together the two panels of the cape, and thereafter keeps it quite closed, holding the edges together with both hands from inside. The man then utters a sentence, already heard a few seconds previously: 'He'll find it, rue Bouvard, he'll find it.' The child looks obstinately down at his boots, the rubber soles of which show as a yellow line at floor level.

So the woman finally yielded? And yet the soldier has not noticed her giving, in his presence, any kind of permission for the child to go out. Might this scene have taken place outside his presence? But where and when? Or is her agreement considered unnecessary? She is standing a little to one side now, in the shadow of the adjacent room, framed in the open doorway. She is quite still, arms hanging rigidly down beside her body. She is silent, but no doubt she has just said something, which is what might have drawn the soldier's gaze in that direction. Her dress, too, is different: she no longer wears an apron over her grey, full skirt. Her face has the same dead-pan expression, but is softer perhaps, more distant. The darkness makes her eyes look larger; across the table with its empty glass she is staring at the child, himself motionless in the dark cape that conceals him entirely from the neck to the legs; the position of his hands, which are invisible, inside, can be seen by the pinching of the edges of the cape at two different levels, once near the collar and once half-way down.

77

Behind the child the man with the crutch has also ceased to move; he is leaning forward, back hunched, balanced in a way that looks precarious but is made possible by the crutch held at a slant to prop the body and gripped firmly in the hand, arm stretched, shoulder held high, the free arm half bent towards the boy's back, the hand partly open, the index and third fingers almost straight, the others folded back into the palm, which is turned upwards. The expression on his face is set in a kind of smile, a 'friendly smile' perhaps, but because of the stiffness of the features more like a grin; one corner of the mouth curling up, one eye more closed than the other and one cheek puckered.

'He'll find it, rue Bouvard, he'll find it.'

Nobody speaks. The child is looking at his boots. The disabled man is still bent forward as if about to fall, the right arm half stretched out, the mouth distorted by what was once a smile. The woman seems to have stepped further back into the shadow of the adjacent room, and her eyes, looking even larger, are perhaps now turned towards the soldier.

And then the street, the night, the falling snow. The soldier, holding his parcel tight under his arm, both hands deep in his coat pockets, is finding it difficult to follow the boy, who is three or four yards ahead. The flakes, small and close together, are being driven horizontally by the wind, and the soldier, in order to avoid receiving their impact full in the face, bends his head a little more; he also narrows his eyelids as much as is possible without closing them altogether. He can hardly see the two black boots appearing and disappearing alternately below the hem of the coat, advancing and withdrawing on the snow, one after the other.

When he passes into the light of a street-lamp he can see the little white spots rushing to meet him, very clear against the black leather of his boots, and, higher up, clinging to the material of his coat. And as he is himself in the light he lifts his head to try and catch sight of the boy in front of him. But the boy, of course, has already re-entered the shadow; and it is rather the innumerable white flakes that come between them that are illuminated by the street-lamp, so that nothing can be seen beyond them. Soon, blinded by the fine crystals whipping him full in the face, the soldier has to lower his eyes once more to the coat that is gradually whitening with the snow, to the ill-tied parcel, to the big boots that come and go like two pendulums, each marking parallel oscillations, identical but opposite.

It is not until a few steps further, after he has emerged from the halo of light, that he can once again be sure of the boy's presence, an uncertain shadow with its cape flapping in the wind against the brightness of the next street-lamp, five or six yards ahead.

And the boy has disappeared for good. The

soldier is alone; he has stopped in his tracks. It is a street just like the others. The boy brought him this far and left him alone, in front of a house identical to all the others, saying: 'That's it.' The soldier looked at the house, the street, first one side then the other, and the door. It was a door like all the others. The street was long and dark, except for the bright areas here and there under the same cast-iron lamp-posts with the old-fashioned ornaments.

The boy set off at once; but instead of going back the way he had come he went straight on in the same direction. He walked a dozen yards and then suddenly began to run. The flaps of his cape flew behind him. He continued in a straight line, soon vanishing, then reappearing at each street-lamp, vanishing, and so on, getting more and more tiny, shapeless, obscured by the night and the snow. . . .

The soldier is alone, looking at the door before him. Why did the child point out to him this house rather than another, since he had been asked only to bring him to this street? And what street is this? Is it the one they were talking about? The soldier cannot remember the name the disabled man was so keen on: something like Mallart, or Malabar, Malardier, Montoire, Moutardier. . . . No, it didn't sound like that.

On the side of the doorway, the side that receives a little light from the nearest street-lamp, a small plaque is fixed at eye-level: some inscription concerning the tenant of the house, or one of the tenants at least. The light is not sufficient for the soldier to read by. Mounting the step, which is so narrow he can only stand there with difficulty, he feels the plaque with his hand. The letters are deeply engraved on a cold smooth surface, but they are too small and the soldier cannot make out a single word. At this moment he notices that the door is ajar: door, passage, door, hall, door, then at last a lighted room, and a table with an empty glass which still contains a circle of dark red liquid at the bottom, and a disabled man leaning on his crutch, bent forward precariously. No. Door ajar. Passage. Staircase. Woman running up the stairs from floor to floor, right up the narrow coil, her grey apron fluttering round in a spiral. Door. And finally a lighted room: bed, chest of drawers, fireplace, desk with a lamp standing on its left corner, and the lampshade throwing a white circle on the ceiling. No. Above the chest of drawers hangs an engraving framed in black wood. . . . No. No. No.

The door is not ajar. The soldier passes his finger over the smooth plaque, but his hand is already numb with cold and he can no longer feel anything. Then suddenly the door opens wide. The corridor is still the same, but this time it is lit. There is the naked bulb hanging at the end of its flex, the notice about passive resistance on the brown wall just inside the entrance, the closed doors to right and left, and the stairs at the other end, spiralling up towards a succession of walls and dark corners.

'What do you . . . ?'

It is another soldier, or rather half a soldier, for he is wearing an army cap and tunic, but with black civilian trousers and grey suede shoes. Feet and legs slightly apart, eyes wide, mouth half-open, the silhouette stands there speechless, threatening, fearful, then retreats towards the end of the corridor, imperceptibly at first, then faster and faster but without turning round and without the feet changing their position relative to each other, the limbs and body remaining rigid as if the whole were mounted on a rail and pulled by a string from behind. No.

As the soldier, having mounted the narrow step, on which he tries as best as he can to keep some sort of balance, half leaning against the closed leaf of the door, which is rather in his way so that he has to contort himself a little, his left hand still deep inside his coat pocket and the brown paper parcel still held tightly against his side, the other hand raised towards the smooth plaque fixed in the doorway on the wall at the left, as the soldier tries in vain to make out the inscription by feeling it with the tips of his three fingers together, the index, the middle and the ring finger, the door suddenly opens, so swiftly that he has to grab hold of the doorpost so as not to fall, so as not to be snatched into this gaping corridor in the middle of which stands a man, a little way in, a man standing quite still, wearing an army cap and tunic but with civilian trousers and low-cut fancy shoes; no doubt they have rubber soles, for there was no warning sound of steps as he came along the corridor. On the collar of his tunic the two coloured lozenges bearing the army number have been removed. The man is still holding with one hand the edge of the door he has just swung on its hinges. The free, right hand moves up to shoulder-height in a sign of wel-come, which is left unfinished, and then falls back.

'Come in,' he says. 'This is it.'

The soldier crosses the threshold and takes three steps into the corridor, which is lit by a naked bulb hanging at the end of a long and twisted electric flex. The soldier stops. The other man has shut the door. The draught has moved the lamp, which is now swinging slowly at the end of its flex.

The man in the army tunic is quite still again by the closed door, arms and legs slightly apart, hands hanging in an attitude both rigid and indecisive at the same time. All the distinguishing marks of his uniform have been unpicked: not only those on the collar but also the stripes on the sleeves and on the cap, and the spaces they occupied are shown by small areas of newer cloth, softer and more coloured than the neighbouring areas, which are worn out, dirty, and faded by long usage. The difference is so marked that the shape of the absent signs is left in no doubt: the lozenge of the infantry, the two slim, oblique, parallel rectangles indicating the rank of corporal; only the colours are missing (light red, crimson, purple, blue, green, yellow, black . . .) which would give precise information as to the regiment, the duties, etc. The face, now in the full light, seems tired, drawn, thin, with over-prominent cheekbones, greyish cheeks, eyes deep in their sockets. The shadow of the man is projected on the wood of the door, to the right, then to the left, then to the right, to the left, to the right, according to the position of the electric bulb as it swings at the end of its long flex in a direction perpendicular to the line of the corridor. (The draught must surely have swung the lamp longitudinally, but the plane of the oscillations has gradually changed, without their perceptibly diminishing in amplitude, and the fore-shortened shadow of the man appears and disappears now to the right, now to the left, alternately.)

'Are you wounded?' he asks at last.

The soldier makes a negative sign with his head.

'Ill?'

'No . . . Just tired.'

'All right. Up you go.'

But neither of them moves. And the man's shadow goes on swinging. Then he says:

'What have you got there, in that parcel?'

The soldier, after some hesitation, lowers his eyes to the stained brown paper and the distended string.

'Things. . . .'

'What sort of things?'

'Things of mine.'

He raises his head. The man is still gazing at him with the same tired, almost absent look.

'Have you got your military papers?'

'No. . . .' The soldier attempts a smile, or a fleeting grin, which distorts his mouth for a moment; then his eyebrows go up to emphasise his astonishment at this unreasonable demand.

'No, of course,' the other repeats, and after a few seconds: 'That's all right. Up you go.'

At that moment the light goes out. Total darkness replaces the thin wan face, the two hanging hands with their out-spread fingers, the shadow and its pendulum motion. At the same time the timing-mechanism has stopped, the regular ticking of which has been audible, although the soldier has not been conscious of it, since the beginning of the scene.

And it is on a silent scene that the light returns. The décor is apparently the same: a narrow corridor, painted dark brown to half-way up and above that a nondescript beige which also covers the very high ceiling. But the doors, both to the right and to the left, are more numerous. They are, as before, painted dark brown all over, and identical in shape: very tall for their narrow width. The corridor is probably longer. The electric bulb is the same: round, rather dim, hanging at the end of a twisted flex. The light-button, made of white porcelain, is situated just at the top of the stairs, in the angle of the wall. The two men are walking slowly, saying nothing, one behind the other. The first, the one who is wearing a corporal's old tunic, has just pressed the light-button as he went past it (was there no button on the ground-floor, since the stairs were climbed in the

85

dark?); but the restarting of the system makes only a single click; the too-faint sound of the timing-mechanism is drowned by the noise of the big hob-nailed boots on the last few steps, which the soldier climbs with less difficulty now that he can see clearly. His guide, in front of him, has rubber soles to his grey suede shoes; the whisper of his steps is barely audible. The two men, one behind the other, walk past the closed doors to left and right one after another, narrow and high, each with its white por-celain knob, bright against the flat dark paint, a rounded mass shaped like an egg and reflecting the electric bulb in a luminous point repeated on the right and on the left at every door, one after another.

At the very end of the passage is the last door, similar to the others. The soldier sees the man stop ahead of him, his hand on the porcelain door-knob. When the soldier has caught him up the man opens it quickly to let him in first, goes in himself, closes the door behind them.

They are standing in a small room, unlighted except for a bluish gleam coming in from outside through the six panes of a window which has neither shutters nor curtains. The soldier walks up to the bare panes. He sees a deserted street, white with snow, uniformly white. His hand rests on the por-celain handle, which is smooth and cold to the touch. The window is not fastened, the two leaves have just been pushed together, they open of their own accord from the mere weight of the arm on the handle. The soldier leans out. It is no longer snowing. The wind has dropped. The night is quiet. The soldier leans out a little further. He sees the pavement, much further down than he expected it to be. Hanging on to the hand-rail, he sees the vertical row of windows immediately below him, and the front door of the building right at the bottom, and the white door-step lit up by the nearby street-lamp. The door itself, which is slightly recessed, cannot be seen. There are footprints in the fresh snow, a trail made by big boots which comes from the left along past the houses, leads to the front door and ends there, directly below. A vague shape is moving in the doorway. It looks like a man wearing a greatcoat, an army coat possibly. He has climbed up on the step and his body is pressed against the door. But the part of him sticking out is clearly recognisable: a shoulder with a buttoned epaulette, an arm folded round a rectangular parcel the size of a shoebox.

'You don't look too good, you know,' says the man, coming back towards him.

The soldier has sat down somehow, on a chair his hand has found behind him. The man, who had left his side for a moment to go and rummage for something at the other end of the room, comes back carrying a fairly heavy bundle, hard to identify in this lunar half-light: folds of material. . . .

'You don't look too good.'

'I don't know . . .' the soldier replies, passing his hand over his face, 'No . . . It's nothing.' The

87

other hand has remained in his coat pocket. He re-adjusts the parcel in the angle of his elbow. He sees the vertical row of windows, each marked with a white line on the snow-covered window-sill, the vertical row of parallel rungs dropping down and down to the front door-step, like a falling stone. He pulls himself up and mechanically follows the man, who is walking towards the door. They are blankets he has under his arm. In the corridor the time-switch has gone off again.

They are standing in a long room lit with blue bulbs. There is a row of beds on either side against the walls: a bare wall to the left, and to the right a series of equidistant windows with their six panes stuck over with paper. The windows seem to be flush with the wall without the slightest recess; only their darkly painted frames show where they begin; as the wall around them and the paper exactly covering each pane are of the same pale shade in this blue light, the windows could well be fake, just thickly outlined rectangles divided into six by thinner strokes: a vertical stroke down the centre and two horizontals cutting it in thirds. After the total darkness of the corridor the soldier walks without difficulty between the two orderly rows of metal beds; the feeble lighting is sufficient for him to be able to see the outlines of things quite clearly.

There are men lying on almost all the beds, wrapped in dark blankets. The man with the unpicked tabs has led the soldier to the middle of the row on the side of the windowless wall, and assigned him an empty bed, placing the blankets on the straw mattress; and he has gone off, without further explanations, on his rubber soles, and closed the door behind him.

The folded blankets form two dark rectangles against the light background of the mattress, two rectangles that overlap at one corner. The two neighbouring beds to right and left are occupied: two bodies lying on their backs, wrapped in blankets, heads resting on bolsters of the same pale shade as the straw mattresses; the one on the right has in addition placed his hands under his neck so that his elbows are pointing obliquely upwards on either side. The man is not asleep: his eyes are wide open. The one on the left, whose arms are hidden along his body, is not asleep either. Others, further on, are lying on their sides, slightly raised up on their elbows. One of them is even half-sitting: he is looking, in the semi-darkness, at the new arrival, who is standing by his bed, the outstretched fingers of one hand touching the horizontal metal bar at the foot of it, the other hand in the pocket of his coat, a shoebox under his arm. All are perfectly still and silent. No doubt they are not sleepy: it is too early yet; and the lack of sufficient light prevents them from doing anything else except lie there, eyes wide open, looking at the new arrival, who is standing there like a statue, with his shoebox, or at the false windows in front of them, or at the bare wall, or at the ceiling, or into space.

The soldier moves at last to the head of the bed, at the same time taking the parcel from beneath his left arm with his right hand. And he is still again. This room, he now notices, differs from real military barrack rooms in one important detail: there is no baggage shelf along the wall behind the beds. The soldier stands there with the box in his hands, wondering where he is going to put it for the night, afraid to let go of it and to attract yet further attention to it. After much hesitation, he moves the bolster away from the painted metal bars of the bedhead, places the box there, on the end of the mattress, and pushes the bolster back against it, wedging it firmly. He hopes that in this way, when his head is lying on the bolster any attempt to grab the box would wake him up, however heavily asleep he might be. Then, sitting on the bed and bending forward, he starts slowly removing his puttees, rolling the band of material upon itself as he goes, turning it round his leg.

'You don't even know how to wind your puttees.'

At the foot of the street-lamp, on the edge of the pavement, the boy is staring at the soldier's ankles. Then, raising his eyes slowly up the legs, he scrutinises every detail of the soldier's clothing from foot to head, finally resting his gaze on the hollow cheeks, black with beard.

'Where'd you sleep last night?'

The soldier makes a vague sign in reply. Still bending down, he unties a bootlace. The child starts

walking backwards slowly, retreating from the foreground of the scene, but without turning round,
without making the slightest movement, still staring
at the soldier with his serious eyes beneath the navy-
blue woollen beret pulled right down over his ears,
and with his hands holding the edges of the cape
together from inside, as his body seems to glide away
on the snowy pavement, along the flat façades, passing the ground-floor windows one after another:
four identical windows, followed by a door that is
hardly different, then four more windows, a door, a
window, a window, a window, a window, a door, a
window, a window, faster and faster as he gets further
away, becoming smaller and smaller, less and less distinct, more and more vague in the twilight, suddenly
swallowed up near the horizon and vanishing at
once, in a split second, like a falling stone.

The soldier is lying on his straw mattress, fully
dressed, having removed only his big boots which
he has placed under the bed beside his puttees. He
has wrapped himself in the two blankets, over his
coat which he has merely unbuttoned at the collar,
too exhausted to make another movement. The room
is in any case not heated, except by the breathing of
the men gathered there. There is no large, square,
tiled stove near the door at the back, at the end
of the counter, its chimney-stack elbowing at
right angles, climbing up to rejoin the wall above the
bottle shelves. But the main thing is to have found
a shelter from the snow that is falling and the wind.

The soldier, his eyes wide open, continues to stare into the shadows before him, a few yards before him, where the child is standing, stiff and motionless too, arms hanging down his body. But it is as if the soldier cannot see the child—neither the child nor anything else.

He has long finished his drink. He does not seem to be thinking of leaving. And yet, around him, the last customers have left the café, and the proprietor has gone out through the door at the back after turning off most of the lights.

'You can't sleep there, you know.'

Beyond the table and the empty glass, behind the child, beyond the big front window with its gathered curtain veiling the lower half, its three balls forming a triangle and its inscription in reverse, the white flakes go on falling just as slowly, vertically, regularly. It is no doubt this continuous movement, even and unalterable, which the soldier is contemplating as he sits so still at his table between his two companions. The child squatting on the floor in the foreground is also looking in the same direction, although he cannot, without raising his head, see the bare window above the gathered curtain. As for the other characters, they do not seem concerned about what is happening there: the drinkers sitting at the tables and talking with animated gestures, the crowd at the back moving towards the left of the picture where the overloaded coat-stands are lined up, the group standing on the right, facing the wall, reading the notice posted there, and the proprietor behind his counter, leaning towards the six well-dressed men who form a small circle of emphatic postures, caught like all the others in the middle of gestures from which this arbitrary halt has removed all naturalness, like those of a group some photographer has wanted to take 'live' but for technical reasons has had to keep posing for much too long: 'Now! Quite still please. . . .' An arm is half-raised, a mouth half-open, a head thrown back; tension has succeeded movement, features have become stiff, limbs rigid, smiles set tight, the vitality of the moment drained of its sense and meaning. And in their place nothing remains but exaggeration, and strangeness, and death.

The six characters in long jackets and frock-coats standing in front of the counter under the eye of the proprietor, whose massive body leans towards them, arms apart, hands gripping the inside edge of the counter, on top of which are the six full glasses belonging to the customers now temporarily diverted from their thirst by a discussion that is doubtless bubbling over with excitement and noise —a fist threateningly raised, a head thrown back to raise the pitch of the sacred words which the lips are violently pouring forth, and the others all around approving, punctuating the sentence with other solemn gestures, speaking or shouting all at once—

the six characters gathered on the left in the foreground are those who first attract the attention.

But the most noticeable of the group is perhaps not the short, corpulent man declaiming in the middle, nor the four standing around him (two seen from the front, one in profile, one from behind) who echo his speeches, but the last, standing further back, a little apart, and dominating his companions by almost a head. His dress is apparently the same, as far as one can judge since his body is almost entirely hidden by his neighbours except for the collar opening over a wide white cravat, a well-tailored shoulder, and the other arm that reappears behind one of the heads, stretching out horizontally to lean from elbow to hand against the rounded edge of the counter, in front of a glass whose shape is a flared cone on a round base.

He seems to be quite indifferent to what his friends are saying and doing before his eyes. He is looking over the heads of the drinkers seated at the tables towards the only female character in the whole scene: a waitress, whose slender figure is moving about the middle of the room, carrying a tray with a single bottle on it, weaving in and out between the benches, the tables, the chairs and the bodies of seated workmen lounging in all directions. She is wearing a very simple dress with a full gathered skirt, fitted at the waist and with long sleeves. She has abundant hair which she wears in a bun, and regular features, sharp yet delicate. Her posture has

94

a certain grace. It is difficult to tell which way she is going on account of the marked contortion of the bust and the entire body, which results in her profile pointing in a different direction from her hips, as if she were sweeping her eye over the tables to find out if anyone is calling her, holding her tray meanwhile with both hands high above the heads around her. The tray moreover is sloping perilously, as is the litre-bottle balanced upon it. Instead of keeping an eye on her precarious load the woman is looking the other way, her head, in relation to the tray, turned at an angle of more than ninety degrees towards the right half of the scene and the round table where the three soldiers are sitting.

It is not certain that it is they alone who interest her: other customers are in her line of vision at the same time, beyond this particular table, some civilians sitting at another table, less noticeable because more lightly drawn but nevertheless just as much present for the waitress herself. And, as it happens, one of this group seems to be stretching out a hand to call her over.

But the look which the one visible eye of the young woman with the black hair might be directing at this outstretched arm in the background would in any case pass just across the upturned face of the soldier who is presented from the front, framed by his two companions (whose faces are not visible on the drawing); an expressionless face, lined with fatigue, whose calm contrasts with the contortions

95

and grimaces so much in evidence all around. His hands, likewise, rest flat on the table which is covered with an oilcloth of small white and red chequered squares on which glasses, many times picked up and put down, have left many circular marks, some thicker than others, some more complete than others, some drier than others, some more distinct than others, some completely obliterated by the sliding of a glass, or by a coat-sleeve, or by the flick of a rag.

And now the woman is sitting on a chair facing the soldier, on the other side of the table with the red and white oilcloth that hangs down at the edges in stiff folds. As the soldier slowly munches the bread she fetched for him at the same time as she got the bottle and the glass, he looks towards the half-open door at the other end where the silhouette of a child is vaguely discernible. The young woman with the black hair and the light eyes has just asked her questions as to what regiment her visitor belongs to—what regiment, at least, his uniform and military badges belong to.

In the ensuing silence, when the soldier has raised his eyes to look at his hostess, her head turns imperceptibly in an anti-clockwise direction towards the portrait hanging on the wall above the chest of drawers. It is a full-length photograph of her husband, taken on the morning of his departure for the front line, during the first days of the offensive, in the period when everyone at home was convinced that victory would be swift and easy. She has not, since then, received any news of him. She knows only that the unit in which he was serving was somewhere in the area of Reichenfels at the time of the enemy breakthrough.

The soldier asks her what unit it was. Despite her not very precise reply and her complete ignorance of army organisation it seems that the position mentioned by the lady must be an error: the battalion she is speaking of did not even fight; it was encircled and disarmed much further to the west. The soldier, however, has no desire to start a discussion on this point, all the less so as the young woman might perhaps take it as a slight on her husband's military career. He limits himself therefore to a general remark: there were far fewer troops at Reichenfels than was later claimed.

'So you think he was taken prisoner?'

'Yes,' he says. 'Probably.' Which does not commit him much since, if he is not dead, he will in any case be a prisoner soon.

It was at this moment that the disabled man entered the room through the partly-open door leading from the next room, moving without the slightest difficulty between the various obstacles, manoeuvring his wooden crutch with skill. And soon the boy reappeared through the other door.

It is this boy who then leads the soldier through the deserted streets in the gathering dusk, past the houses with their unlighted windows. And yet there are still some people left in the town; a lot of the civilians must somehow not have got out when there was still time. Does no one dare to turn the light on then, in the rooms that face the street? Why do these people continue to obey the obsolete orders about passive resistance? Out of habit, probably; or else because there is no authority to bring back the previous regulations. It would of course be of no importance, not now. The street-lighting in any case is functioning as in peacetime; some street-lamps have even been alight all day.

But from the windows that follow in succession along the flat façades, on the ground-floor as on every floor of the high, uniform houses, there filters not a glimmer of light. And yet not a single shutter or curtain is closed either outside or inside the panes, which are as black and bare as if all these flats were uninhabited, and which shine only occasionally, at certain fleeting angles, with the brief reflection of a street-lamp.

The boy seems to be going faster and faster and the soldier is too exhausted to keep up with him. The slight figure, wrapped in its black cape, from beneath which emerge the two black, narrow-trousered legs, draws further and further ahead. Every instant the soldier fears he has lost sight of it. Then he glimpses it far in front, much further on than where he was looking, suddenly lit up as it passes a lamp-post, then re-entering the darkness, invisible once more.

The child could at any moment turn off into an

adjacent street without being seen, for the route he has chosen is far from straight. Fortunately the fresh snow on the pavement retains his footprints, the only ones on the whole immaculate surface between the line of the house fronts and the parallel edge along the gutter, footprints which are very clear despite the speed of his progress, quite shallow in the thin new layer which has just fallen, covering the paths hardened by passers-by during the day, prints of chevroned rubber soles with a cross inside a circle on the heel.

Now the trail stops suddenly in front of a door exactly like the others but with one leaf not completely shut. The step that forms its threshold is very narrow and can be crossed without the foot touching it. The end of the corridor is lit. The noise of the timing-mechanism can be heard, like the ticking of a cheap alarm-clock. In the continuation of the corridor a narrow staircase begins, rising in short flights separated by small, square landings and elbowing at right angles. The landings on each floor, in spite of the many doors giving out on to them, are hardly wider. Right at the top is the closed room where the dust is gradually accumulating in a grey layer on the table and on the small objects scattered upon it, on the mantelpiece, the marble of the chest of drawers, the divan and the polished floor where the felt slippers. . . .

The trail continues, regular and rectilinear, in the fresh snow. It continues for hours, a right foot, a left

99

foot, a right foot, for hours. And the soldier goes on walking, mechanically, numb with fatigue and cold, advancing one foot after another, machine-like, without even being certain of making any progress, for he keeps finding the same regular footprints in the same places beneath his feet. And since the space between the chevroned soles corresponds to his own stride, the stride of a man at the end of his tether, he has begun quite naturally to place his feet in the marks made before him. His boot is a little larger but this is hardly noticeable in the snow. He has the feeling, suddenly, of having already passed there himself, before himself.

But the snow was still falling at that time in massed flakes, and the footprints of his guide were hardly made before they began already to lose their precision, filling up quickly, becoming less and less recognisable as the distance increased between him and the soldier, their very presence itself soon becoming doubtful, the slight depressions barely perceptible in the evenness of the surface, finally disappearing completely over several yards. . . .

The soldier thinks he has definitely lost the trail when he sees the boy waiting for him a few steps away under a street-lamp, wrapped tightly in his black cape which is already white with snow.

'That's it,' he says, pointing to the door, which is exactly the same as the others.

Then comes the electric bulb swinging at the end of its long flex, and the shadow of the man swinging on the door he has just closed, like a slow metronome.

The soldier wakes up in the night with a start. The blue lights that hang from the ceiling are still burning. There are three of them, on the line of the room's main axis. In one movement the soldier has thrown off his blankets and sat up on the edge of the bed with both feet on the floor. He was dreaming that the alert had sounded. He was in a winding trench, the top of which was on a level with his forehead; in his hand he was holding a sort of elongated grenade whose delayed-action mechanism he had just set off. Without wasting a second he had to throw the thing out of the trench. He could hear the noise of the timing-mechanism, like the ticking of a cheap alarm-clock. But he just stood there, grenade in hand, his arm stretched out as at the beginning of a throw, but for some incomprehensible reason paralysed, becoming more and more rigid, less and less capable of moving even a finger as the moment of the explosion approached. He must have yelled aloud to jerk himself out of the nightmare.

And yet the other sleepers look quite peaceful. Probably he did not actually shout. On closer scrutiny he notices that his neighbour's eyes are wide open : his two hands under his neck, he continues to stare into the shadows before him.

Partly with the intention of finding a little drinking water, partly to save face, the soldier gets up and, without putting on his boots so as not to make a noise, emerges from the row of beds and walks towards the door he came in by. He is thirsty. Not only does his throat feel dry but his whole body seems to be on fire, despite the cold. He reaches the door and tries the handle, but it resists. He dares not shake the handle too much for fear of waking everybody up. Besides, the door seems to be locked.

He turns, panic-stricken, and notices that the windows, the false windows painted in black on the wall, are now on the left, whereas they were on the right when he entered this room for the first time. Then he notices another identical door at the other end of the long aisle between the two rows of beds. Realising his mistake, he re-crosses the room, this time along its whole length, between the two lines of prostrate bodies. Every eye is wide open and watches him pass in complete silence.

Indeed, the other door opens easily. The washroom is at the end of the passage. The soldier inquired about that on the way up, before going to bed. Wishing to adjust the position of the brown paper parcel under his arm, he suddenly remembers he has left it behind his bolster, unguarded. He closes the door at once and walks quickly back towards his bed. He can see at a glance that the bolster is now pushed right back against the vertical bars; he moves closer to the bed, and realises that the box is no longer there; he turns the bolster over, as if further proof were necessary, he turns the bolster over, twice; finally he straightens up, not knowing what to do. But neither are there any blankets on the mattress. And the soldier recognises, three beds further along, some blankets thrown back in a heap on an empty mattress. He has merely got the wrong bed.

On his own bed everything is in place : blankets, bolster and parcel. And underneath the bed the boots and the rolled puttees are also there. The soldier gets back in, without his drink of water. Despite his burning throat he no longer has the strength to start on another journey, to go through the maze of unlighted corridors towards that infinitely distant and problematical water. His comings and goings through the dormitory have been performed very rapidly, in the overspill of agitation from his feverish awakening. Now he feels incapable of taking another step. He could not, in any case, go out carrying the big box without arousing, or reinforcing, pointless suspicions; he has already attracted too much attention by his recent behaviour. In no time at all he has wrapped his feet and legs in one of the blankets and lain down again, spreading the second blanket over his body as best he can. And once more he is walking in the snow along the deserted streets beneath the high flat façades that succeed one another, without variation, indefinitely. His route is punctuated by black lamp-posts with stylised ornaments anachronistic in their elegance, whose bulbs burn with a yellow glare in the bleak daylight.

The soldier hurries as much as he can without

actually running, as if he is afraid, at one and the same time, that someone is pursuing him, but that a too-obvious flight will arouse the suspicions of the passers-by. But there is not a silhouette of a passer-by visible, for as far as the eye can see, down to the grey extremity of the rectilinear street, and each time the soldier turns to look behind him, without stopping or even slowing down his pace, he can see that there is no pursuer threatening to catch him up: the white pavement stretches on, as empty in this as in the other direction, with only the line of footprints left by the hob-nailed boots, a little distorted here and there, in each place where the soldier has looked round.

He was waiting at the corner of a street near a lamp-post. He was looking straight ahead of him, at the corner house on the other side of the road. He had been looking at it for some time before he noticed that some people were gathered in a room on the second floor. It was a fairly large room with no visible furniture, and it had two windows; the silhouettes came and went from one to the other, but without nearing the glass panes which were bare of curtains. The soldier saw mainly their pale faces, withdrawn in the obscurity of the room. The room must have had very dark walls for these figures to detach themselves so clearly against a background of shadow. The people seemed to be talking among themselves, consulting one another; they were making gestures, indicated by the relative whiteness of their hands. They were watching something in the street and the subject of discussion seemed to be of some importance. Suddenly the soldier understood that it could only be himself: there was nothing else where they were looking, on the pavement or in the road. To mislead them he began to examine his surroundings, scrutinising the horizon first in one direction, then in the other. Not exactly to mislead them but to show them that he was waiting for some-one and was not in the least concerned about the house in front of which he happened thus by chance to find himself.

When he glanced again, furtively, up at the second-floor windows the pale faces had quite clearly come much nearer to the bare panes. One of the people was coolly pointing a finger at him; the other faces were grouped around the first at varying levels, as if their owners were some of them slightly crouch-ing, others on the contrary raised on tiptoe, or even standing on chairs; the neighbouring window was empty.

'They think I'm a spy,' the soldier thought. And preferring not to have to face this accusation, which looked as if at any moment it might take a more pressing form, he pretended to consult a non-existent watch on his wrist and moved away without further reflection up the perpendicular street.

After a dozen steps he condemned this behaviour as clumsy: it could only have confirmed the sus-picions of the observers, who would soon be hot on his trail. Instinctively he walked more quickly. In fact, thinking he heard behind him the noise of a window being violently thrown open, he could hardly keep himself from breaking into a run.

The soldier turns once more to look behind him : there is still no one. But then, as he brings his eyes back to the direction of his progress, he sees the boy apparently watching out for him, half-hidden behind the corner of a building at the next crossroads.

This time the soldier stops dead. The door of the building on his left is ajar on a dark entrance. Up at the crossroads the boy has gradually moved back until he is entirely hidden behind the quoin. The soldier makes a sudden jump sideways and finds himself in the corridor. At the end of it, without wasting a minute, he starts going up the successive flights of narrow stairs elbowing at right angles and separated by small, square landings.

Right at the top, on the last floor, is the room, all shut in behind its thick curtains. The box wrapped in brown paper is lying on the chest of drawers, the short bayonet on the marble mantelpiece. There is already a thin layer of dust on the stout, double-edged blade, dulling its shine in the filtered light that comes from the shaded lamp on the table. The shadow of the fly on the ceiling continues its manoeuvres.

On the right of the big luminous circle whose circumference it follows with regularity, in the angle of the ceiling and the wall, there is a little black line, very fine, some four inches long, barely discernible: a crack in the plaster, or a cobweb laden with dust, or the mark of some blow or scratch. This imperfection in the white surface is however not equally visible from all angles. It is particularly noticeable for an observer against the right wall, but low down against the wall and at the other end of the room, looking upwards at an angle, more or less following the diagonal of this wall, as is natural for a person lying on the bed with his head on the bolster.

The soldier is lying on his bed. Probably it is the cold that has woken him up. He is on his back, in the same position as when he opened his eyes; he has not moved since. In front of him the windows are wide open. On the other side of the street there are other windows, identical with these. Inside the room all the men are still in bed; most of them seem to be asleep. The soldier has no idea how long he himself has slept. Nor does he know what time it is now. His immediate neighbours to right and left are wrapped as tightly as possible in their blankets; one of them, who is turned towards him, has even covered up part of his face, leaving only his nose showing, with a corner of the blanket over his head protecting his eyes like a visor. Difficult though it is to see what the sleepers are wearing, it seems that none of them has undressed for the night, for nowhere are there any clothes hanging, or folded, or thrown about.

There are in any case no coat-stands or shelves or cupboards of any description, and only the ends of the beds could be used to hang up any coats, tunics, trousers, etc. . . . ; but these bed-ends, consisting of metal bars painted with white gloss, are all completely bare, at both ends of each bed. Without moving his body the soldier feels the bolster behind him to reassure himself that the box is still there.

He must now get up. If he does not succeed in delivering this parcel to the person for whom it is meant, he can at least get rid of it while there is still time. Tomorrow, this very evening, or even in a few hours' time, it will be too late. In any case he has no reason to remain here doing nothing; his prolonged stay in this pseudo-barracks, or sick-bay, or reception-centre, can only produce new complications for him, and he may be compromising his last chance of success.

The soldier tries to raise himself on his elbows. His whole body is stiff and heavy. Having only managed to slide up a few inches towards the bed-head he lets himself fall back, his shoulders leaning now against the vertical metal bars that support the thicker, horizontal one on which his neck now rests. There is no danger, fortunately, of crushing the box. The soldier turns his face to the right, in the direction of the door through which he must go out.

Beyond the man whose face is hooded by a corner

of the thick brown blanket, the next sleeper has an arm sticking out of his blankets, an arm clothed in khaki-coloured cloth : the sleeve of an army tunic. The hand, which is reddish, is hanging over the edge of the mattress. Further on other bodies are lying, prostrate or curled up. Several have kept their forage caps on.

At the end of the room the door has opened noiselessly and two men have come in, one behind the other. The first is a civilian, dressed like a farmer : rough leather boots, tight riding breeches, a canvas jacket with a fur collar open on a long roll-neck sweater; he has kept his hat on, a faded felt hat, shapeless with wear; his whole outfit is generally worn out, baggy, and even rather dirty. The second character is the man from the previous evening, wearing his tunic and his corporal's cap with the stripes unpicked. Without stopping at the first beds, not even glancing at them as they pass, they have moved down the central aisle to one of the sleepers in the row opposite, under the second window. At the foot of the bed the two men talk together in low voices. Then the civilian in the felt hat approaches the bed and touches the body in the region of the shoulder. At once the blanketed torso shoots up and a dead-white face appears, with eyes sunk in their sockets and hollow cheeks blackened by a beard of several days' growth. Wrenched from his sleep with such a start, the man takes a little while to get his bearings, as the other two stand motionless by him.

He passes a hand over his eyes, across his fore-head, into his short and greyish hair. Then he starts swaying and suddenly falls back on the mattress.

The civilian must be some sort of doctor or medical orderly, for he then carefully picks up the man's wrist and holds it between his fingers for a certain time as one does to measure the pulse, but without, however, consulting a watch. He then lays the inert arm along the prostrate body. He exchanges a few more words with his companion; after which they cross the room together diagonally, to the patient with the very red hand sticking out of the blankets and hanging over the edge of the mattress. Leaning forward so as not to have to move the sleeping man's arm, the orderly picks up this hand, like the previous one, without here causing the slightest reaction. The examination lasts a little longer this time and the two men then have a longer conversation in low voices. Finally they move away from the bed, without having woken the patient.

The orderly then gazes slowly round the rest of the room; he stops at the newcomer, who, unlike his fellow-patients, is half sitting up on his bed. The corporal with the unpicked stripes makes a sign with his chin to point him out and says something like: 'Arrived last night.' They come nearer. The corporal remains at the foot of the bed, the other comes up to the head; automatically the soldier offers his wrist, which the orderly grasps with a firm gesture without asking anything. After a few seconds he states flatly, as if talking to himself:

'You have a temperature.'

'It's nothing much,' says the soldier; but his own voice surprises him, weak and off-pitch.

'A very high temperature,' the man says again, letting go of his wrist.

The hand falls back, inert, on the mattress. The corporal has taken a black notebook from his pocket and is writing down with a very short pencil information which the soldier thinks he can easily guess: the date and time of his arrival, the army number from the collar of his greatcoat, this number twelve thousand three hundred and forty-five which has never been his.

'How long?' asks the orderly in the felt hat.

'How long have I been here?'

'No: since you started running a temperature.'

'I don't know,' says the soldier.

The man rejoins his colleague and they turn towards the windows for a brief discussion which the soldier cannot hear, nor can he guess it from their lips because he cannot see their faces. But the orderly comes back to him; he leans over him and presses with both hands, through the many thicknesses of clothing, on the sides of his chest:

'Does that hurt, when I press?'

'No . . . not specially.'

'And you slept like that?'

'How do you mean: like that?'

111

'In a wet coat.'

The soldier feels the stiff, rough material himself: it is still a little damp. He says:

'Must be the snow. . . .'

His sentence is so indistinct that it disintegrates before it is finished; he even wonders afterwards whether he really uttered it.

The orderly now speaks to his colleague:

'He ought to change.'

'I'll see if I've got something,' the other says. And at once he makes for the door with his silent step.

Left alone, the orderly buttons up his canvas jacket, which is the colour of earth, faded and stained in front, with three buttons of plaited leather which he passes through their loops one after the other; all three are very worn, and the bottom one has a wide gash in the centre of the rounded part: a strip of leather a quarter of an inch long has come loose. The orderly has put both hands in the baggy side-pockets. He looks at the soldier for a moment and asks:

'Aren't you cold?'

'No . . . Yes . . . A little.'

'We can shut the windows now,' the man says. And without waiting for the soldier's opinion he walks to the left-hand end of the dormitory to close the end window. From there he moves along the wall to the right, slipping between the wall and the iron bars of the bed-heads, and repeats the performance, coming nearer and nearer, pushing the windows to and manipulating the fastenings, which he has to force, several times. As he goes the daylight decreases in the big room, the darkness gaining on him from the left and becoming more and more dense.

There are five windows. Each has two leaves divided into three panes. But these panes are only visible when the window is wide open, for they are covered on the inside with dark paper which is barely translucent and is stuck over the whole surface of the glass. When the man has finished the entire room is plunged into semi-darkness, the five rectangular openings replaced by five sets of six mauvish squares, vaguely luminous, diffusing a glow similar to that of the blue night-lights, and all the more insufficient in that it follows without transition upon the bright daylight. The man in the canvas jacket and the felt hat, standing at the right-hand end of the room near the exit, is no more than a black silhouette, motionless against the lighter wall.

The soldier thinks the visitor will now leave the room, but on the contrary he comes towards his bed: 'There,' he says. 'You'll be less cold.' And after a silence: 'He's going to bring you some other clothes. But you must stay in bed.'

He is silent again; then he adds: 'In a little while the doctor will come, this afternoon perhaps, or later this morning, or in the evening. . . .' He speaks so low at times that the soldier can hardly understand.

'Meanwhile,' he continues, 'you will take the

tablets they give you. . . . You mustn't . . .' The end of his speech is lost. He has taken a pair of large fur gloves from his pocket and he puts them on slowly, still adjusting them as he moves away. A few yards further on nothing remains of him but a vague shadow; and even before reaching the door he has disappeared completely. Only his heavy boots can be heard moving away with slow steps.

Now it is no longer light enough to distinguish the attitudes of the sleeping men. The soldier realises this will make it easier to leave the room without being seen. He will go and have a drink on the way in the washrooms at the end of the corridor.

He makes another effort to raise himself and this time he manages to sit up, but still leaning on the metal bar behind him. To achieve a more comfortable position he lifts the bolster up behind his back and places it on top of the box. Then he leans over to the right, stretching his hand to the floor in search of his boots. At this moment he notices a black silhouette in front of him, the head and upper body of which are outlined against the luminous squares of mauve paper. He recognises the man who received him the previous evening, the corporal with no stripes, wearing his forage cap. The right hand returns to its place on the mattress.

The man puts something down on the iron crossbar at the foot of the bed, something that looks like a greatcoat, an army coat possibly. Then he moves forward between the two beds, up to the soldier, holding out a glass which is three-quarters full of a colourless liquid.

'Drink,' he says. 'It's water. There are some tablets at the bottom. Later you'll get some coffee, when the others get theirs.'

The soldier takes the glass and drinks greedily. But the half-dissolved tablets which he swallows with the last mouthful get stuck, and there is no water left to help them down. The bitter, granular dregs remain in his throat, stinging the mucous membrane. He feels even more thirsty than before.

The man has taken back the glass. He is looking at the whitish trails left on the sides. Finally he goes, indicating the foot of the bed:

'I've brought you another coat,' he says. 'You will put it on before you lie down again.'

An indeterminable length of time after his silent shadow has vanished the soldier decides to get up. He swings his legs round carefully and sits up on the edge of the bed, knees bent, feet resting on the floor. His whole body gradually subsides and he pauses for a long time, or so at least it seems.

Before continuing his manoeuvre he disentangles himself from the blankets, throwing them aside on the mattress. Then, leaning further forward, he lets his two hands hang down towards the floor; he is groping for his boots; finding them by touch he puts them on one after the other and starts lacing them up. The mechanical gestures come back to him as he winds on his puttees.

But he experiences considerable difficulty in getting to his feet, as if the weight and bulk of his body had become those of a deep-sea diving-suit. Then he begins to walk, a little more easily. Taking care not to clatter his hob-nailed boots on the wooden floor, he emerges from the row of beds and after only a few seconds' hesitation turns right towards the door. He immediately changes his mind and comes back to examine the coat left by the corporal. It is the same as his own, just about. Perhaps a little less worn. On the collar, the distinguishing mark of the regiment— a lozenge of felt with the number—has been unpicked, on both sides.

The soldier replaces the garment on the end of the bed and gazes at it in the dark, his mind empty, supporting himself with one hand on the horizontal metal bar. At the other end of the bed he sees the box, still under the bolster. He goes back to the bedhead, rolls the bolster over, takes the box, places it under his left arm. As he touches his own coat, he feels the dampness of the thick material. He puts both hands into his pockets. The lining is cold and wet.

Stopping again near the dry coat, at the same spot as before, he waits a little longer before leaving. If he exchanges his coat for this one he will not need to unpick the red felt lozenges on his collar. He takes his hands out of his pockets, puts the box down on the bed, slowly unbuttons his coat. But he cannot easily remove his arms from the sleeves, his shoulders are so stiff at the joints. When he has finally managed it he allows himself a short rest before continuing the operation. The two coats lie side by side on the metal bar. He must, in any case, put one of them on again. He picks up the new one and slides in his arms quite easily, fastens the four buttons, takes up the box again, replaces it under his left arm, plunges both hands into his pockets.

This time he has not forgotten anything. He walks stealthily towards the door. At the very bottom of the right pocket his fingers encounter a round hard object, smooth and cold, the size of a big marble.

In the corridor, where the light is on, he meets the corporal, who stops to watch him pass and is apparently on the point of saying something when the soldier goes into the washroom—normal behaviour after all: the corporal may well think he has taken the parcel because it contains his toilet things.

When he comes out again, having drunk a great deal of cold water from the tap, the corporal has gone. The soldier goes on his way, along the transverse corridor towards the stairs which he begins to descend slowly, holding on to the banister with his right hand. Although he watches his movements carefully the stiffness of his knees makes his progress both heavy and automatic and the clatter of his big boots resounds on the wooden stairs, one after the other. The soldier stops at each landing, but as soon

as he starts to go down again the noise of his hob-
nailed boots on the steps recommences, regular,
weighty, solitary, echoing through the whole building as through an empty house.

At the foot of the stairs, by the last step of the
last flight, the disabled man is standing, supported by
his wooden crutch. The crutch is slanting forward
against the step; the whole body is leaning in
apparently precarious equilibrium; the face is upturned, set in an unnatural smile of welcome.

'Hello,' he says. 'Slept well?'

The soldier has now stopped too, his parcel under
one arm, the other hand on the banister. He is
standing on the edge of the first half-landing, seven
or eight steps higher than the disabled man. He
answers:

'All right,' in an uncertain voice.

In this position the disabled man is barring his
passage. The soldier would have to move him aside
in order to walk down the last step and towards the
street-door. He wonders whether this really is the
same character he met in the light-eyed woman's flat,
the same man who in fact told him of the existence
of this pseudo-barracks for the sick. If he is not the
same, then why has this man addressed him is if he
knew him? If he is the same, how can he have come
so far as this on his crutch, through streets covered
with frozen snow? And for what purpose?

'Is the lieutenant up there?'

'The lieutenant?'

'That's what I said—the lieutenant! Is he there?'

The soldier hesitates. He moves nearer the banister to prop himself up against it. But he does not want to make too apparent his extreme fatigue, and he holds himself as stiffly as possible and articulates as clearly as he can:

'What lieutenant?'

'The one in charge of the place, of course!'

The soldier realises that he had better pretend to know whom the man is talking about.

'Yes,' he says, 'he's up there.'

He wonders how the disabled man will manage the stairs with his crutch, which he generally uses with such skill. Perhaps he stopped at the bottom of the stairs because it is impossible for him to climb them. He does not, in any case, attempt the slightest gesture for the time being, and merely continues to stare at the soldier without either making way for him or coming up to meet him.

'I see you've unpicked your number.'

The smile on the upturned face has become more pronounced, twisting the mouth and the whole of one side of the face.

'Oh, you're quite right,' the man goes on: 'You never know—better be cautious.'

In order to cut short the conversation, the soldier decides to take a pace forward himself. He goes down one step, but the disabled man has not moved an inch so that the second foot, which had remained behind, now comes to rest beside the first instead of reaching down to the next step.

'Where are you going now?' the disabled man goes on.

The soldier shrugs evasively:

'Got things to do.'

'That box of yours—what's in it?' the disabled man asks.

Continuing down the stairs, this time without stopping, the soldier grunts an irritated reply: 'Nothing interesting.' When he reaches the man he leans back suddenly against the banister. With a swift movement the disabled man moves his crutch and steps aside towards the wall. The soldier passes in front of him and continues along the corridor. He knows without turning round that the disabled man is following him with his eyes, leaning forward on his crutch.

The front door is not locked. As he manipulates the handle the soldier hears a jeering, vaguely threatening voice behind him: 'You're in a hurry this morning.' He goes out and closes the door. The engraved metal plaque in the doorway reads: 'Headquarters, Military Depots, North and North-West Regions.'

The cold in the street is so intense that it grips him. He feels nevertheless that it is doing him good. But he would need to be sitting down. He has to be content with leaning his back against the stone wall, his feet on the strip of fresh snow left between the row of houses and the yellowish path trampled by the passers-by. In the pocket of the coat his right hand feels the large, hard, smooth marble.

It is an ordinary glass marble about an inch in diameter. The surface is perfectly regular and highly polished. Inside it is quite colourless and absolutely transparent except for an opaque kernel, the size of a pea, at the centre. This kernel is black and round; whichever way the marble is turned it looks like a black disc about an eighth of an inch in radius. The solid mass of clear glass all around it contains only unrecognisable fragments of the red and white design of which it occupies a circular fraction. Beyond this circle the chequerboard pattern of the oilcloth covering the table continues in all directions. Moreover the surface of the marble reflects the café scene, paler, distorted, considerably reduced.

The child is rolling the marble on the red and white chequered oilcloth, gently, careful to avoid giving it sufficient momentum to carry it beyond the limits of the rectangular field. It crosses the rectangle diagonally, rolls down the long side, returns to its point of departure. Then the child picks it up and looks at it for a long time, turning it round and round. After which he gazes at the soldier with his large, serious eyes:

'What is that inside?' he says in his too-deep voice, which is not the voice of a boy.

'I don't know. Glass too, probably.'

'It's black.'

'Yes. It's black glass.'

The child re-examines the marble and asks again:

'Why?' And when the soldier does not reply he repeats: 'Why is it in there?'

'I don't know,' says the soldier. Then, after a few seconds: 'To make it pretty, I expect.'

'But it's not pretty,' says the child.

He has lost almost all his mistrust now. And although his voice is still serious, almost adult in tone, he talks with a youthful simplicity, sometimes even with naïve enthusiasm. He is still wearing his black cape over his shoulders but he has taken off his beret, revealing very short, fair hair with a parting on the right.

This boy is the one from the café, it seems, who is not the same as the other one who led the soldier (or who will be leading him, later on) to the barracks—from which, as a matter of fact, he has brought the marble. It is this boy, at any rate, who brought the soldier into the café run by the big, burly, silent man, where he has drunk a glass of red wine and eaten two slices of stale bread. He feels less weak after this meal. And so, to thank the child, he has made him a present of the glass marble found in the pocket of his coat.

'You're really giving it to me?'

'Yes, I told you.'

'Where's it come from?'

'From my pocket.'

'And before?'

'Before? Before, I don't know,' says the soldier. The child shoots him a curious look, slightly incredulous probably. He immediately takes on something of his old reserve and it is in a much colder tone on voice, with his eyes fixed on the collar of the coat, that he observes:

'You've unpicked your number.'

The soldier tries to take this with a smile:

'It's not much use now, you know.'

The child, however, does not smile. He seems to find the explanation unsatisfactory.

'But I know it,' he says. 'It was twelve thousand three hundred and forty-five.'

The soldier does not answer. The boy goes on:

'Is it because they're coming today that you took it off?'

'How do you know they're coming today?'

'My mother . . .' the boy begins; but he goes no further. For something to say the soldier asks:

'And she lets you hang about the streets?'

'I don't hang about: I was on an errand.'

'Was it she who sent you?'

The child hesitates. He looks at the soldier as if to guess what might follow, where he is being led, what sort of trap is being laid for him.

'No.' he says at last, 'not her.'

'Your father, then?' the soldier asks.

This time the boy does not make up his mind to answer. The soldier has himself been speaking more

123

slowly during this last interchange. The slight stimulation caused by the wine has passed already. Now his exhaustion is slowly gaining the upper hand. Probably he still has a temperature; the effect of the tablets did not last long. He continues, nevertheless, in a more hollow voice :

'I met him this morning, I think, coming out of the barracks. He certainly gets around with his bad leg. Yes, I think it was him. So he wasn't at home . . .'

'It wasn't my father,' says the boy.

And he turns his head towards the glazed door.

The two workmen at the next table have interrupted their conversation, possibly some time ago. The one who had his back turned has pivoted on his chair, without letting go of his glass or lifting it from the table, and he has remained in this position, his body half twisted round to look over his shoulder towards the soldier, or towards the child. The latter has moved away. At least, he is now a fair way from the soldier, over to the left, near the wall where the white notices are posted up announcing the evacuation of the town by the troops. Complete silence has fallen in the room.

The soldier has remained in the same position : both elbows on the oilcloth, his two forearms laid our flat in front of him, his two hands, stained with grease, drawn a little towards each other, separated by a distance of about eight inches, the right hand still holding the empty glass.

The proprietor, a tall silhouette of burly stature, has re-entered the scene behind his bar on the extreme right. He too is standing quite still, a little bent, leaning forward, arms apart, hands gripping the edge of the counter. He too is looking at the soldier, or at the child.

The child has put his beret on again; he has pulled it down very low on both sides so as to cover his ears as much as possible, and he has closed his cape around his body, holding it with both hands from inside. At the other end of the café the proprietor has not moved either. When he served the soldier a while ago he told him that when he had seen him through the window, and then coming in, he had taken him, in this town where no more soldiers were to be seen and where the newcomers were expected hourly, he had taken him for one of them. But this had been due only to his surprise, and once the soldier had come in the proprietor had immediately recognised the familiar uniform with the long coat and the puttees.

The boy had then closed the door behind this unexpected customer. The proprietor at his post, the well-dressed customer standing beside the counter, the two workmen sitting at their table, all followed him with their eyes, saying nothing. It was the boy who broke the silence with his deep voice that was so unchildlike that the soldier thought he was hearing one of the four men who had watched him come in. The boy was still near the door at that point, behind the soldier's back. But the others in front of him remained quite motionless, mouths shut and lips still; and the sentence, without anyone appearing to have uttered it, seemed to be a caption under an engraving.

Afterwards the soldier, his glass of wine finished, did not linger further in the silent café. He picked up his parcel from under his chair and left the room, accompanied to the door by the stares of the proprietor and the two workmen. After quickly readjusting the slack white string he replaced the brown paper parcel under his left arm.

Outside, the cold has again taken him by surprise. This coat cannot be as thick as the other one, unless perhaps the temperature has dropped considerably during the night. The snow, hardened by repeated footsteps, crunches under the nails of his boots. The soldier walks quickly to get warm; carried along by the regularity of this noise he is making himself as he walks, he moves forward with eyes lowered along the deserted streets as if at random. When he had decided to continue on his way it was because he had been spurred on by the idea that there was still some possibility of delivering the box to the person for whom it was meant. But once on the pavement again, after closing the café door, he no longer knew which direction to take: he tried simply to go towards the place of the first missed rendezvous, without moreover pausing to reflect on the best way to get there, since the man would no longer be waiting for him there anyway. The soldier's only hope is that the man lives somewhere around there and that he might meet him on the way. At the first intersection he came across the disabled man.

As he approaches the crossing where, just at the corner of the last house, this character is standing, he realises that it is not the disabled man but the well-dressed man who was drinking at the counter a while ago; he is leaning not on a crutch but on a rolled umbrella which he is holding out in front of him, pointing it into the hard snow, his body leaning forward slightly. He has little spats over his polished shoes, very narrow trousers and a short coat, probably lined with fur. He has no hat on his balding head. A little before the soldier reaches him the man bows in a rapid greeting, his umbrella remaining poised at an angle in front of him. The material of the umbrella, which is tightly rolled, is protected by a black silk sheath.

The soldier answers with a slight nod and is about to pass on, but the other makes a gesture with his free hand and the soldier assumes that the man is going to say something. He turns towards him and stops, raising his eyebrows with the look of someone who is waiting for someone else to speak. At this point the man, as if he was not expecting this, lowers his eyes towards the end of his umbrella, which is planted at an angle in the hardened and yellowed snow. He keeps his left arm half-raised, however, with elbow bent, hand open, thumb sticking upwards. On his fourth finger he is wearing a large signet ring bearing a grey stone.

'Filthy weather, isn't it?' he says at last. And he turns his head towards the soldier. The latter thus feels justified in waiting: he has the impression, again very clear, that this short sentence is to serve as a prelude to disclosures of a more personal kind. He answers merely with a vaguely acquiescent noise, a sort of grunt. But he still waits to hear the rest.

A considerable time elapses, however, before the man with the umbrella and the fur-lined coat makes up his mind to ask: 'Are you looking for something?' Is that the signal?

'I was to meet . . .' the soldier begins.

As the rest is so long in coming the man finishes the sentence himself:

'Someone you have missed?'

'Yes,' says the soldier. 'It was yesterday . . . The day before, rather . . . It was for midday. . . .'

'And you arrived too late?'

'Yes . . . No: first I must have got the wrong place. An intersection . . .'

'Was it a crossroads like this one? Under a lamp-post?'

A black lamp-post, its base surrounded with a garland of stylised ivy whose contours are emphasised by the snow. . . . At once the soldier corroborates with more detailed explanations; but, once started, he is seized with doubt, so that he now prefers, out of caution, to limit himself to a series of disconnected phrases, that is to say with no apparent link, most of them unfinished and in any case extremely obscure to the other man, and in which he himself becomes more and more confused at every word. The other man makes no sign, listening merely with a polite expression, his eyes slightly crinkled, his head inclined to the left, showing neither understanding nor astonishment.

As for the soldier, he does not know how to stop. He has drawn his right hand from his pocket and is holding it out with fingers tensed, like a man afraid of losing some detail he thinks he is on the point of fixing in his memory, or like a man who wants a little encouragement, or who feels he is failing to convince. And he goes on speaking, losing himself in a superabundance of increasingly confusing details, entirely aware of it, almost stopping after every phrase, only to take off again on a new tack, convinced now, too late, of having blundered from the start and seeing no way of extricating himself without giving rise to even worse suspicions in this anonymous stroller who had only wanted to speak of the weather or some equally harmless subject, or even perhaps wanted nothing of him at all—and who in any case persists in remaining silent.

While struggling in the meshes of his own words the soldier tries to reconstruct what has just occurred; an impression must have crossed his mind (incredible though it now seems) that the man he had been pursuing since his arrival in the town was, per-

haps, this very one, with his umbrella in its silken
sheath, his fur-lined coat, his large signet ring. He
had wanted to allude to what he had hoped of him
and, while not revealing his true mission, nevertheless to allow the man to guess it if he really were the
person for whom the box wrapped in brown paper
was meant, or at least the one who was to tell him
what to do with it.

The man in the small grey spats and black polished
shoes was, on the contrary, giving no sign of con-
nivance. The be-ringed hand had even been lowered
again and plunged into the pocket of his coat. The
right hand, the one holding the knob of the
umbrella, is gloved in dark grey leather. The soldier
thought, for a moment, that this person was remaining silent on purpose: that he was in fact the person
for whom the parcel was meant but was refusing to
make himself known, that having learnt what he
wanted to know he was now concealing his
identity. . . . It was absurd, of course. Either he had
nothing to do with this business, or he had not yet
taken in what the soldier was trying to tell him,
which did in fact concern him in the highest degree.
And since he had not, at the first words spoken,
grasped the hint that was being offered to him, the
soldier had to choose between two solutions: to
speak more frankly, or to go immediately into
reverse. But he had not had time to opt for one or the
other and had stuck to going in both directions
at once, a method which moreover ran the risk

of putting the man off if he had after all, been, etc. . . .

The soldier must finally have stopped talking, for now they are once again facing each other dumbly, frozen in the same positions as they occupied at the beginning: the soldier has both hands in his coat pockets and is looking slightly sideways at the man in the fur-lined coat, whose left hand, ungloved, and ornamented with a signet ring bearing a grey stone, is half-raised, while with his right he is holding at arm's length his umbrella, which is pointing forward at an angle in the hard snow of the pavement. Behind him, about three yards away, stands a cast-iron lamp-post, an ancient gaslamp with old-fashioned ornaments, equipped now with an electric bulb that shines with a yellowish glare in the dull daylight.

The man has however gleaned some information from the soldier's inconsistent and inchoate mumblings for, after reflecting for a while, a fairly long while probably, he asks:

'So someone was to meet you then, not far from here?' And he adds a moment later, as if to himself: 'A man in the street, during the last few days.'

Then, without waiting for further confirmation or making any other relevant query, he begins to tell how he himself has in all likelihood seen the person in question: a man of medium size, bare-headed, wearing a long brown coat and standing by a lamp-post a few streets away, almost in front of the door of

131

a corner house. He had seen him several times—
twice at least—as he was passing nearby: that morning, and the previous day, and perhaps also the day
before that. This solitary character, dressed entirely
in dark brown, standing with his feet in the snow,
for a long time, judging by his position—leaning
with hip and shoulder against the cast-iron column
like a man tired of standing up—yes, he certainly
remembered having seen him.

'What sort of age?' the soldier asks.

'In his thirties . . . forties, perhaps.'

'No,' says the soldier. 'That wasn't him. He would
have been over fifty and dressed in black. . . . And
why would he come back like that, several days
running?'

This last argument has no great validity, he
realises, since he himself in fact came back several
times—this morning too—to what he supposed to
be the place—that was in any case variable—of the
rendezvous. Besides, his interlocutor suggests that a
change in the expected clothing may well have been
imposed by the snow which was falling heavily at that
time; as to the age, he cannot be sure of it, having
seen the silhouette from some distance away, particu-
have been me you saw.'

'In that case,' says the soldier, 'it could just as well
have been me you saw.'

But the man assures him he would not have confused an infantry uniform with a civilian outfit. He
is insistent and persuades the soldier to make the

132

detour to the place in question and at least glance at it: it is so near as to be worth the trouble, especially if the matter is important.

'That box you're holding under your arm, you were telling me that . . .'

'No,' the soldier interrupts. 'It has nothing to do with it.'

Since there is practically no alternative left to him he decides, despite his certainty as to the uselessness of such an undertaking, to go to the crossroads in question: he must turn right at the third intersection, then walk to the end of the block, or else to the street after. He has made off without turning round, leaving behind him the stranger leaning on his umbrella. This protracted halt has chilled him to the bone. Although his joints feel numb with fever and fatigue it is a relief to be walking again, all the more so towards a goal that is both precise and not too distant. Having confirmed the vanity of this last hope, which is not even a hope, all he will have to do is to get rid of his cumbersome parcel.

The best thing would clearly be to destroy it, or at any rate the contents, since the box itself is made of metal. But although it would be a simple matter to burn the papers it contains or to tear them into small shreds, there are other objects inside more difficult to break up—the exact nature of which he has in any case never examined. He will have to get rid of the whole thing. The simplest solution from every point of view would be to throw away the parcel without undoing it. Just then, as he is crossing a transverse street, the soldier sees the mouth of a drain just in front of him near the rounded corner of the pavement. He goes up to it and, overcoming his stiffness, crouches down to check that the box is not too high to be pushed under the arched opening cut into the kerb. Fortunately the layer of snow is not so thick as to hamper the operation. The box will just make it. It will need only to be pushed in horizontally and tipped down. Why, for that matter, not throw it away at once?

At the last moment the soldier cannot do it. Having satisfied himself—twice, even—that the thing could easily be achieved, he stands up again and prepares to continue on his way, to see first whether there, by some chance . . . But the simple prospect of having to step up the kerb, which is about eight inches high, stops him for almost a minute, so exhausted is he by his recent pitiful efforts.

As soon as he stops moving the cold that grips him becomes unbearable. He steps over the drain on to the pavement and takes two more steps. Suddenly his fatigue is such that he can go no further. He leans with hip and shoulder against the cast-iron column of the lamp-post. Was it not here he had to turn off to the right? Wondering whether the man with the grey ring has perhaps remained standing where he was, leaning forward on his umbrella, in order to direct him from afar as to the turning he has to take, the soldier glances over his shoulder. Twenty paces away, advancing in his tracks, is the boy.

The soldier turned his head away at once and has started walking again. After five or six steps he looks back a second time. The boy is following him. If he could, the soldier would break into a run. But he is at the end of his tether. And probably the child means him no harm at all. The soldier stops and turns round once more.

The boy has also stopped and is staring at the man with his serious wide-open eyes. He is no longer wearing his beret; nor is he holding his cape tightly shut in front of him.

Now the soldier is walking towards the boy, almost without moving his body, taking slow steps, as if benumbed. The boy makes no movement of withdrawal.

'Have you got something to tell me?' the soldier asks, in a voice he would have liked to sound threatening, and which barely gets past his lips.

'Yes,' the boy replies.

But he says nothing further.

The soldier looks at the snow-covered step two yards to his left in front of a closed door. He would feel the cold less if he huddled into the doorway. He takes a step. He murmurs:

'Well, I'm going to sit down for a bit.'

Reaching the door he leans in the corner, half against the wood, half against the stone wall.

The boy has pivoted round to follow him with

his eyes. He has opened his mouth a little. He looks
first at the face, which is dark with beard, then at
the body slumped backwards, the parcel, the big
boots slightly apart at the foot of the step that marks
the threshold. Slowly the soldier lets himself slide
down against the door, bending his knees, until he is
sitting in the snow that has piled up on the narrow
step in the right-hand corner of the doorway.

'Why were you throwing away your box?' says the
child.

'No, no . . . I wasn't going to throw it away.'

'What were you doing then?'

His deep voice is now without mistrust, his questions are not ill-meant.

'Just looking to see,' says the soldier.

'To see? . . . To see what?'

'If it went through the opening.'

But the child does not look convinced. He grips
the edges of his open cape, one in each hand, and
swings his arms rhythmically backwards and forwards, forwards and back. The cold still does not
seem to bother him. At the same time, without coming any nearer, he continues his careful scrutiny:
the brown parcel now held in place between the
chest and thighs, the coat collar with the unpicked
badges, the folded legs with the knees pointing up
through the flaps of khaki material.

'Your coat,' he says at last. 'It's not the same as
yesterday.'

'Yesterday. . . . You saw me yesterday?'

'Of course. Every day I've seen you. Your coat was dirty. . . . Did they take off the stains?'

'No . . . Yes, if you like.'

The child pays no attention to the reply.

'Your puttees,' he says. 'You don't know how to wind them.'

'Good . . . You can teach me.'

The boy shrugs his shoulders. The soldier, for whom this dialogue is too much, is nevertheless even more afraid of seeing his companion run off, abandoning him in the deserted street where night will soon be falling. Was it not this boy who took him to a café that was open, and to a barracks dormitory? The soldier forces himself to ask in a more pleasant voice:

'Was that what you wanted to tell me?'

'No,' the boy answers. 'That wasn't it.'

Then they heard the sound, very far away, of the motorbike.

No. It was something else. It is dark. It is another attack: the sharp, staccato sound of automatic rifles, now close by, now farther off behind the copse, and occasionally from the other side too, against a duller background rumbling. The earth of the path is now as soft as after ploughing. The wounded man is becoming heavier and heavier, he can hardly manage to lift up his boots, can hardly walk any more. He has to be supported and dragged along at the same time.

They have both abandoned their packs. The wounded man has also left his rifle behind. But he has kept his; its strap has just given way so that he has to hold the gun in his hand. He should have taken another; there was no shortage of rifles. He prefers to keep the one he is used to, which in addition to being useless is also cumbersome. He is carrying it by the middle, horizontally, in his left hand. With his right he is holding the waist of his wounded comrade, whose left arm is flung around his neck. They stumbled at each step in the soft earth lined with transverse furrows and ridges in the darkness that is lit up now and then with fleeting glows.

Then he is walking alone. He has no bag, no rifle, no comrade to support. He is carrying only the box wrapped in brown paper under his left arm. He is moving forward into the night, over the fresh snow that covers the ground evenly, his steps leaving footprints one by one in the thin layer with the regular sound of a metronome. At the crossroads, under the yellow light of the street-lamp, he approaches the gutter and bends down, one foot on the road, the other on the pavement. Between his stiff outspread legs is the stone arch of the mouth of a drain; he bends his body further forward and holds out the box towards the black opening, into which it vanishes at once, swallowed up by the void.

The next picture is of a barracks dormitory or more precisely the dormitory of a military sick-bay. The rectangular box, the shape and size of a shoebox, is lying on the baggage-shelf next to an aluminium mug, a mess-tin, some khaki clothes folded in an orderly manner and various small objects. Below, in the white-painted metal bed, a man is lying on his back. His eyes are closed; the eyelids are grey, as are the brow and temples, but the two cheekbones are touched with bright pink; over the hollow cheeks, around the half-open mouth and on the chin the very dark beard is at least four or five days old. The sheet which covers him to the neck rises and falls regularly with the wounded man's slightly wheezy breathing. A reddish hand protrudes from the brown blankets at one side and is hanging over the edge of the mattress.

To right and left, other bodies are lying on other identical beds ranged in rows against the bare wall along which, three feet or so above the heads, is fixed the shelf laden with packs, wooden trunks, folded clothes, khaki or greenish, and aluminium mess-kits. A little further on, among some toilet articles, stands a large round alarm-clock, which has probably stopped, which says a quarter to four.

In the next room a considerable crowd is gathered: men, most of them in civilian clothes, standing and talking in small groups with a great deal of gesticulation. The soldier tries to push his way through, but without success. Suddenly, a person he had seen only from behind, barring his way, turns round to face him and stands quite motionless staring at him through slightly narrowed eyes as if he were concentrating hard. One by one the people all round also turn to look at him and are suddenly frozen, silent, their eyes a little narrowed. He is now in the centre of a circle which becomes gradually larger as the silhouettes move back, leaving only their pale faces still visible, getting further and further apart, at equal intervals, like a line of lamp-posts along a rectilinear street. The row sways slowly into place to form a receding perspective. The black cast-iron columns are clearly outlined against the snow. In front of the nearest one stands the boy, watching him with wide-open eyes:

'Why are you sitting like that?' he says. 'Are you ill?'

The soldier makes an effort to answer:

'It'll pass.'

'Have you lost your barracks again?'

'No . . . I'm going back now.'

'Why aren't you wearing your forage cap? All soldiers have caps . . . or helmets. . . .'

After a pause the child goes on, in a still lower voice: 'My father's got a helmet.'

'Where is he, your father?'

'I don't know.' Then, vehemently, articulating each word clearly: 'It's not true he deserted.'

The soldier looks up at the boy:

'Who says he deserted?'

By way of reply the child performs a few lame steps, one leg stiffened, one arm stretched down the side of his body holding a crutch. He is now only a yard from the door. He says again:

'But it's not true. He also said you're a spy. You're not a real soldier: you're a spy. Inside your parcel there's a bomb.'

'Well, that's not true either,' says the soldier.

It was then that they heard the sound, very far away, of the motorbike. The boy was the first to prick up his ears; he opened his mouth a little wider and his head swung round slowly from lamp-post to lamp-post towards the very end of the grey street, already dim in the gathering dusk. Then he looked at the soldier, and back towards the end of the street, while the noise grew faster and faster. It was definitely the vibration of a two-stroke engine. The child stepped back towards the doorway.

But the noise began to decrease, soon becoming almost inaudible.

'Must get back,' said the child.

He looked at the soldier and repeated: 'Must get home.'

He came up to the soldier and held out his hand. The soldier, after a moment's hesitation, grasped the hand and managed to get up, hoisting himself with his shoulder against the door.

The same engine vibration started up again, in the silence, this time increasing much more markedly. The man and the boy stepped back together towards the door. The sound was soon so close that they climbed up on the step and flattened themselves against the wood, side by side. The din, like a pneumatic drill, reverberating from all directions against the houses, was quite definitely coming from the adjacent street, the one forming the crossroads ten yards from their hiding-place. They huddled even further into the doorway. The motorbike appeared level with the vertical wall at the corner of the house. It was a combination with two helmeted soldiers up; they were moving forward slowly in the middle of the road over the untouched snow.

The two men can be seen in profile. The driver's face, in front, is higher than that of his companion on the lower level of the sidecar. They both have much the same features: regular, drawn, perhaps lined with fatigue. Their eyes are hollow, their lips tight, their skin greyish. The coats, in shape and colour, are like those of the familiar uniform, but the helmet is bigger, heavier, coming very low over the ears and neck. The machine itself is dirty, half-covered with dry mud, and looks like a fairly old model. The man who is driving sits quite rigid on the driving seat, his two gloved hands gripping the handlebars. The other looks alternately to left and right down the road ahead, almost without moving his head. He has a black machine-gun on his lap and its barrel sticks out beyond the steel frame of the sidecar.

They passed without turning round and went straight on across the crossroads. Some twenty yards further on they disappeared behind the corner of the house opposite.

142

A few seconds later the noise suddenly stopped. The engine had evidently been turned off. Total silence followed the uproar. Nothing was left but the two parallel lines made in the snow by the three wheels of the vehicle, drawn perfectly straight across the field of vision between the two vertical stone quoins.

As this silence was lasting too long the boy lost patience and came out of his hiding-place. The soldier did not notice immediately, for the child had been snuggled behind him; the soldier suddenly saw him in the middle of the pavement and beckoned him back. But the boy risked three more steps forward to get behind the lamp-post, which was supposed to conceal him.

The silence continued. The boy, who was getting bolder as time went on, moved a few yards further towards the crossroads. Afraid that he might himself attract the attention of the invisible motor-cyclists, the soldier did not dare call him to prevent him from going farther. The child continued until he reached the place from which the transverse street could be seen; venturing forward only with his head he peered round the corner where the combination had vanished. A man's voice, some distance away in that direction, yelled out a brief command. With a jump the boy turned round and began to run; he passed in front of the soldier, the flaps of his cape flying behind his shoulders. Quite unconsciously the soldier had already started following him when the two-stroke engine revved up again, filling the streets at once with its explosions. The soldier too began to run, heavily, just as the child turned the corner into the next street.

The din behind him soon became deafening. Then a long scraping noise was heard : the motorbike taking a corner too fast and skidding on the snow. At the same time the engine suddenly stopped. The hard voice cried out: 'Halt', twice, without a trace of an accent. The soldier was nearly at the corner of the street into which the child had turned a few seconds before. The motorbike started up again, drowning the powerful voice that shouted 'Halt' a third time. And at once the soldier recognised the sharp, staccato crackle of the machine-gun mingling with the racket.

He felt a violent blow on the heel of his right boot. He went on. Bullets hit the wall near him. Just as he was turning the corner there was another burst of fire. A sharp pain pierced his left side. Then everything stopped.

He was out of range, protected by the wall. The crackle of the machine-gun had ceased. The engine had probably been switched off a little before. The soldier could no longer feel his body, he kept on running along the stone wall. The door of the building was not closed, it opened of its own accord when the soldier pushed it. He went in. He closed it again gently; the latch made a slight click as it shot home.

Then he lay down on the floor in the dark, curled

144

up, with the box in the hollow of his belly. He felt the back of his boot. There was a deep gash, running down across the upper and the side of the heel. The foot itself was untouched. Heavy steps and loud voices echoed in the street.

The steps were coming nearer. A muffled bang sounded against the wood of the door, then the voices again, harsh, almost jovial, speaking an incomprehensible language with a drawled intonation. He heard one pair of footsteps move away. The two voices, one very near, the other a little further off, exchanged three or four brief sentences. There was a sound of banging, on another door probably, and then on this one again, with a fist, several times over, but in a sort of half-hearted way. The more distant voice shouted out some foreign words again, and the voice nearby began to laugh vigorously. The two laughs then answered each other.

And the two pairs of heavy footsteps began to move away in consort, accompanied by shouts and bursts of laughter. Just as silence was returning the noise of the motorbike started up again, then gradually diminished until it finally became inaudible.

The soldier wanted to alter his position, a sharp pain pierced his side, a pain that was violent but not unendurable. He was more tired than anything else. And he wanted to vomit.

Then he heard the boy's deep voice quite near him in the dark, but he could not understand what it was saying. He felt himself losing consciousness.

In the room a considerable crowd is gathered: men, most of them in civilian clothes, standing and talking in small groups with a great deal of gesticulation. The soldier tries to push his way through. At last he reaches a less congested area where the people are sitting around tables, drinking wine and arguing, also with many movements of the hands and exclamations. The tables are very close together and it is still difficult to move between the benches, the chairs and people's backs; but one can see better where one is going. Unfortunately all the seats seem to be occupied. The round, square or rectangular tables are placed anyhow, in no discernible order. At some of them three or four drinkers are seated; the longer tables with benches can seat over a dozen. Beyond them is the counter behind which the proprietor is leaning, a tall and burly man made more remarkable still by his slightly elevated position. Between the counter and the last few tables, the centre of a very narrow space is obstructed by a group of standing customers who are more comfortably dressed in short town coats or fur-collared cloaks, and whose glasses, placed in front of the proprietor just within their reach, are partly visible in the vacant spaces that remain here and there between the torsos and the gesturing arms. One of these characters, standing a little apart to the right, instead

146

of joining in the conversion with his friends, is leaning back against the edge of the counter looking at the room, the seated drinkers, the soldier.

The latter spots at last, not far away, a small table that is relatively easy of access and occupied only by two other soldiers: a corporal and a bombardier. The one is as still and silent as the other, and their reserved bearing is in strong contrast to everything around them. Between them there is a free chair.

Having managed to reach it without too much difficulty, the soldier puts one hand on the back of the chair and asks if he may sit down. It is the corporal who replies: they were with a friend, who left for a minute, but does not seem to be coming back; perhaps he has met someone he knows elsewhere; meanwhile the soldier can take his place. Which he does, glad to have found a seat where he can rest.

The other two say nothing. They are not drinking; they do not even have glasses in front of them. The hubbub all around them in the room seems not to reach their ears, nor does the agitation reach their eyes, which are staring into space as if the men have fallen asleep without closing their eyelids. Or, if they are awake, it is certainly not the same spectacle that they are gazing at so persistently, for the one on the right is facing the left-hand wall, which is completely bare at that point since the white notices are pinned up further along, and the other is facing in the opposite direction towards the counter.

Half-way to the counter, over which the proprietor's massive torso is leaning forward between
his outspread arms, a young waitress is weaving in
and out between the tables carrying a loaded tray.
Or at least she is trying to pick out the spot she will
be making for: stopped for the moment, she is pivot-
ing round so as to look in all directions; but she
moves neither her legs nor her feet, nor even hardly
her hips under the full gathered skirt, but only her
head, with the black hair drawn back in a heavy bun,
and also her bust a little; even her two outstretched
arms, holding the tray at eye-level, keep it in an
almost fixed position as she faces the other way,
remaining thus contorted for some time.

From the direction of her gaze the soldier thinks
she has noticed him and will therefore approach him
as a new arrival to take his order, or even to serve
him at once, for she has a bottle of red wine on her
tray, tilting it in fact rather dangerously so that it
may at any moment fall from its support, the
horizontal position of which she is so careless about
maintaining. But underneath, in the direct line of
the imminent fall, an old workman's bald head seems
quite unaware of the danger, its owner continuing to
berate the man sitting on his left, or exhort him, or
solicit his agreement, all the while brandishing a
full glass in his right hand, nearly spilling the
contents.

The soldier then realises there is not a single glass
on his own table. On the tray there is only this one

bottle, and nothing else for satisfying a new customer. Besides the waitress has not seen anything of interest to her in his sector and her eye continues to sweep round the room, passing over the soldier and his two companions, now taking in the other tables along the wall where the small white notices are stuck up, each with four drawing-pins, now the front window covered up to eye-level with its gathered curtain and the three enamel balls in low relief on the outside of the pane, then the door, also partly veiled and bearing the word 'café' written backwards, then the counter, with the five or six well-dressed men standing in front of it and, at the extreme right, the last one of this group, who is still looking over towards the soldier's table.

The soldier draws his eyes back into the axis of his own chair. The bombardier is now staring at the coat-collar, at the place where the two lozenges of green felt bearing the army number are sewn.

'So,' he says, 'you were at Reichenfels?' At the same time his chin juts out in a quick pointing movement, over almost before it has begun.

The soldier acquiesces: 'Yes, I was in the wings somewhere.'

'You were there,' the bombardier corrects him, repeating his gesture, by way of proof, towards the badges that distinguish the regiment.

'So was the other chap,' says the corporal, 'who was sitting here before. . . .'

'Yes, but he fought,' the bombardier interrupts.

Then, having obtained no reaction; 'There were some apparently who didn't hold out.'

He turns towards the corporal, who makes a vague gesture of ignorance, or of appeasement.

'Nobody held out,' says the soldier.

But the bombardier protests : 'Some of them did! You ask the fellow who was sitting here before you.'

'All right, all right,' the soldier admits. 'It depends what you mean by "holding out".'

'I mean just that : there were some who fought, and there were some who didn't.'

'They all ended up running away though.'

'Under orders! Mustn't confuse the two.'

'Everyone ran away under orders,' says the soldier.

The bombardier shrugs his shoulders. He looks at the corporal as if hoping for his support. Then he turns towards the big window giving out on the street. He murmurs:

'Lousy officers!'

And again, after a few seconds : 'Lousy officers, that's what it was.'

'Very true,' the corporal agrees.

The soldier is trying to see over to his right or further back, whether the young waitress has decided to come towards them. But even though he has half risen out of his chair to look over the heads of the surrounding drinkers he cannot see her anywhere.

'Don't worry about him,' says the corporal. 'When he comes back, you'll see him.' He smiles at him in a fairly friendly way and adds, still under the impression that the soldier is looking out for their absent companion: 'He must be next door in the billiard-room. He must have found a mate of his.'

'You can ask him,' says the bombardier, nodding his head. 'He fought, he did, you can ask him.'

'All right,' says the soldier, 'but he's here now all the same. He had to retreat too, like everyone else.'

'Under orders, I tell you,' and after a moment of silent thought he concludes, as though for himself: 'Lousy officers, that's what it was!'

'Very true,' the corporal agrees.

The soldier asks:

'Were you there, at Reichenfels?'

'Well, no,' the corporal replies. 'We were more to the West, both of us. We fell back so as not to be taken when they broke through the line from behind.'

'Under orders, mark you! Mustn't confuse the two,' says the bombardier.

'We moved fast,' says the corporal. 'Couldn't drag behind. The twenty-eighth on our left flank waited too long. They were picked up like schoolboys.'

'Anyway, now,' says the soldier, 'it comes to the same thing. Sooner or later we'll all be picked up.'

The bombardier gives him a quick glance, but prefers to address an imaginary person sitting on the other side:

'That's not for sure. We're not finished yet.'

It is the soldier's turn to shrug his shoulders. This time he stands up to try and attract attention and at

151

last get something to drink. From the next table he happens to hear a sentence thrown out in a louder voice in mid-conversation: 'Spies, but they're everywhere!' Relative silence follows this declaration. Then from the other end of the same table comes a longer commentary in which only the verb 'to shoot' can be distinguished; the rest is lost in the general hubbub. And another phrase emerges just as the soldier has sat down again: 'There are some who fought, and there are some who didn't.'

The bombardier is again gazing at the green lozenges on the coat-collar. He repeats: 'We're not finished yet.' Then, leaning towards the corporal, as if in confidence: 'Enemy agents, I've heard, paid to undermine morale.'

The other is silent. The bombardier waits in vain for an answer, leaning forward over the white and red chequered oilcloth, and finally sits up straight again on his chair. A little later he adds: 'We'll see,' but without elaborating his train of thought, and so quietly as to be barely audible. Both of them are now silent and still, each gazing straight in front of him into space.

The soldier has left them in the hope of finding where the young woman with the heavy dark hair is hiding. Now that he is standing up, however, among the scattered tables, he finds that he is not all that thirsty after all.

He is on the point of going out, and has almost reached the counter and the group of well-dressed men, when he suddenly remembers the soldier who had also been at Reichenfels and who had fought so gloriously. The only thing that mattered was to find him, talk to him, make him tell his story. At once the soldier retraces his steps across the room, between the benches, the chairs and the backs of drinkers seated at the tables. Those other two are still alone, in the precise position in which he left them. Instead of going up to them he cuts across towards the back, reaching an area where everyone is standing up: a crowd of men, pushing and jostling each other, making towards the left but moving very slowly because of the narrowness of the passage, which they are nevertheless gradually approaching, between a jutting piece of wall and three huge, circular coat-stands, overloaded with clothes, standing at the end of the counter.

While he too is advancing at the speed of the crowd—slower, even, through being on the edge of it—the soldier wonders why it suddenly seemed so urgent to speak with this man, who will be able to describe nothing that he does not know already. Before reaching the next room where, among another lot of tables, must be a billiard table hidden under a protective sheet, the waitress with the black hair, and the hero of Reichenfels, he has given up his plan.

It is probably here that the scene occurs of the silent crowd moving apart in all directions around him, leaving the soldier alone at last in the centre of a huge circle of white faces. . . . But that scene leads to nothing. Besides, the soldier is no longer in the middle of a crowd either silent or noisy; he has left the café and is walking along the street. It is an ordinary sort of street: long, rectilinear, lined with identical houses with flat façades and uniform doorways and windows. It is snowing, as usual, in small, slow, massed flakes. The pavements are white, as are the road, the window-sills, and the door-steps.

When the leaf of a door is not quite closed the snow, chased into the aperture by the wind during the night, has blown through the narrow vertical crack and leaves a moulding of it when the soldier opens the door wide. A little snow has even accumulated inside, forming a long trail of decreasing thickness on the floor, widening at first and narrowing later, partly melted in any case, leaving a damp black edge all round it on the dusty wood of the floorboards. Other black smudges punctuate the corridor, some eighteen inches apart and becoming more blurred as they approach the stairs, the first steps of which can just be made out at the other end. Although the shape of these smudges varies and is uncertain, being fringed here and there with indeterminate areas, there is every reason to believe that they are marks of footprints left by small shoes.

The corridor is flanked on either side by doors at equal intervals and alternating regularly, one to the right, one to the left, one to the right, etc. . . . The whole pattern continues as far as the eye can see, or almost, for the first steps of the staircase are just discernible, at the end, in a brighter light. A small silhouette, that of a woman or a child, looking quite tiny at such a distance, is leaning with one hand on the large white ball at the end of the banister.

The more the soldier advances, the more this figure seems to retreat. But on the right one of the doors has opened. There, moreover, the trail of footprints stops. Click. Darkness. Click. Yellow light illuminating a narrow entrance hall. Click. Darkness. Click. The soldier finds himself once again in the square room furnished with a chest of drawers, a table and a divan. The table is covered with a chequered oilcloth. Above the chest of drawers a photograph of a soldier in battledress hangs on the wall. Instead of being seated at the table, drinking wine and slowly chewing his bread, the soldier is lying on the bed; his eyes are closed, he seems to be asleep. Around him three people are standing quite still looking at him without speaking: a man, a woman and a child.

Right by his face, at the head of the bed, the woman is leaning forward slightly, scrutinising the sleeper's drawn features, listening to his laboured breathing. The boy is further back near the table, still wearing his black cape and his beret. The third person, at the foot of the bed, is not the disabled man with the wooden crutch but the older man with the balding crown, in the short fur-lined town coat and the polished shoes protected with small spats. He has kept his fine grey leather gloves on, the one on the left hand bulging, on the fourth finger, with the stone of the ring. The umbrella must have remained in the hall, leaning at an angle against the coat-stand, with its ivory knob and its silk sheath.

The soldier is lying on his back, fully dressed, with his puttees and his big boots on. His arms lie along his body. His coat is unbuttoned; the tunic underneath is stained with blood on the left near the waist.

No. It is in fact another wounded man who occupies the scene, at the exit of the crowded café room. The soldier has hardly closed the door when he sees a young fellow-soldier come up to him, a conscript of the previous year whom he came across several times during the retreat and this very morning at the hospital, and who is now himself about to enter the café. For a fraction of a second the soldier imagines that the man before him is the courageous fighter they were speaking of, the one whose behaviour was praised just now by the bombardier. At once he realises the impossibility of such a coincidence: the young man was indeed at Reichenfels at the time of the enemy attack, but in the same regiment as himself as can be seen from the green lozenges on his uniform; and this unit did not include a single hero, as the bombardier only too clearly implied. The soldier is about to pass his comrade with a mere nod when the man stops to speak to him:

'Your mate,' he says, 'the one you went to see this

morning at the surgery, he's in a bad way. And he's asked for you several times.'

'All right,' says the soldier. 'I'll go back there.'

'Be quick, then. He won't last long.'

The young man already has his hand on the brass handle when he turns to add:

'He says he's got something to give you.' After a moment of thought: 'He's just delirious, I expect.'

'I'll go and see,' says the soldier.

He starts off at once, quickening his pace and taking the shortest route. The décor he passes through is no longer that of the symmetrical, monotonous town with its ruler-drawn streets cutting each other at right angles. And there is no snow as yet. The weather is even rather mild for the time of year. The houses are low, of an old-fashioned style, vaguely baroque, over-ornamented with scrolls and moulded cornices, columns with carved capitals framing the doors, balconies with sculptured corbels and complicated bulging ironwork for railings. All this is more or less in harmony with the lamp-posts at the street-corner, former gaslamps now converted, each consisting of a cast-iron column widening at the base and supporting a lyre-shaped construction some ten feet from the ground, with curlicue points from which hangs the glass globe containing the enormous electric bulb. The column itself is not smooth but on the contrary encircled by many rings, varying in shape and size, emphasising at different heights the changes of girth, expansions, contractions, ball- and spindle-shaped bulges; these rings are particularly numerous towards the top of the cone that forms the base of the whole affair; around this cone winds a garland of stylised ivy, moulded in the metal, and repeated identically on every lamp-post.

But the hospital is just a military building of classic construction, set back behind a vast, bare, gravelled courtyard, separated from the boulevard and its leafless trees by very high railings, the gate of which stands open. The sentry-boxes on either side are empty. In the middle of the huge courtyard a man is standing, an N.C.O., wearing his belted tunic and his cap; he has stopped, he appears to be thinking; his dark shadow is outlined at his feet on the white gravel.

As for the room where the wounded man lies, it is an ordinary dormitory, with the metal beds painted white—another scene that leads to nothing, unless it be to the box wrapped in brown paper that lies on the baggage shelf.

So it is armed with this box that the soldier walks through the snowy streets, past the high flat façades, as he looks for the place of the rendezvous, hesitating between several similar crossroads, thinking that the description he has been given is very inadequate for him to be able to recognise the exact spot with any certainty in this large town that is too geometrically laid out. And he ends up, once more, going into a building that looks inhabited, pushing open a door that has been left ajar. The corridor, painted dark brown on the lower half, has the same deserted look as the streets outside: doors without mats or visiting cards pinned up, the absence of those small utensils left here or there for a few minutes that are the usual signs of life in a house, and totally bare walls, with the solitary exception of the regulation notice about passive resistance.

And it is then the side door opens on a narrow entrance hall where the umbrella sheathed in black silk is leaning against a coat-stand of the ordinary type.

But there is another exit, through which it is possible to leave the building without being seen by anyone who watched one come in: it gives out on the transverse street, at the end of a secondary corridor perpendicular to the first and on the left of the staircase that terminates it. This street is in any case similar to the first in every way; and the boy is there at his post, waiting for the soldier at the foot of the lamp-post to lead him to the army offices that are being used more or less as barracks or sick-bay.

They have set out, at any rate, with that intention. But there are more and more crossroads, and sudden changes of direction, and retracing of steps. And the interminable night march goes on. As the boy is going faster and faster the soldier soon cannot keep up with him and finds himself alone once more, with no other expedient but to seek some sort of shelter in which to sleep. He has very little choice and opts resignedly for the first open door he sees. It is again the flat of the young woman in the grey apron, with the pale eyes and the deep voice. And yet he had not noticed, at first, that the room where he was given wine and bread, under the framed photograph of the husband in battledress that decorates the wall above the chest of drawers, contained a divan as well as the rectangular table covered with a chequered oil-cloth.

At the top of the wall opposite this bed, almost in the corner of the ceiling, there is a small black line, very thin and winding, four inches long or a little more, which is perhaps a crack in the plaster, perhaps a cob-web laden with dust, perhaps a smear in the whitewash, emphasised by the crude lighting from the electric bulb that hangs at the end of its naked flex, that swings at the end of its flex like a slow pendulum. At the same rhythm, but in the opposite sense, the shadow of the character with the unpicked stripes and the civilian trousers (is he the one the disabled man called the lieutenant?), the shadow, fixed at the ground, oscillates to right and left against the closed door, on either side of the still figure.

This pseudo-lieutenant (but the missing badges of rank on his tunic were those of a corporal, their traces still clearly visible on the brown material), this man who was receiving the lost, the wounded or the sick like this must previously have leant out of a first-floor window, preferably the one directly above the door, in order to try and make out in the darkness who was asking to be let in. This, however, does not solve the main problem: how had he known that somebody was at the door? Had the boy on arrival knocked on the closed door? So the soldier, catching up with his guide at last after a long delay since for some time now he had been following only his trail, was quite unaware that his presence had already been announced. And as he perched on the narrow step trying to read the inscription engraved on the polished plaque, feeling it over and over again with his fingertips, the host, ten feet above, could see in detail one side of the coat jutting out of the doorway: a shoulder, a soiled sleeve folded over a parcel that looked, in size and shape, like a shoebox.

Not a single window, however, was lighted, and the soldier had thought that this house, like the others, had been deserted by its inhabitants. When he pushed open the door he had quickly perceived his mistake: tenants still lived there in large numbers (as they did, no doubt, everywhere else) and appeared one after the other on all sides, a young woman crouching at the very end of the corridor in the angle of the stairs, another woman suddenly opening her door on the left, and a third, finally, on the right, giving access, after some hesitation, to the entrance hall that once again leads into the square room where the soldier is now lying.

He is lying on his back. His eyes are closed. The

eyelids are grey, as are the brow and temples, but the two cheekbones are touched with bright pink. Over the hollow cheeks, around the half-open mouth and on the chin the very dark beard is at least four or five days old. The sheet which covers him to the neck rises and falls regularly with the slightly wheezy breathing. A reddish hand, stained with black around the knuckles, is sticking out at one side and hanging over the edge of the bed. Neither the man with the umbrella nor the boy is any longer in the room. Only the woman is there, sitting at the table, but at a slight angle so as to face the soldier.

She is knitting a black woollen garment; but her work is not very advanced as yet. The big ball of wool is beside her on the red and white chequered oilcloth, the sides of which fall round the table, making large stiff folds at the corners, the shape of inverted cornets.

The rest of the room is not exactly as the soldier remembers it; apart from the divan which he had hardly noticed on his first visit, there is at least one other important thing to point out: a high window now entirely concealed by tall red curtains hanging from the ceiling to the floor. The divan, although a wide one, could well have passed unnoticed, for it stands in the corner behind the door that would hide it from anyone entering the room; afterwards the soldier sat with his back to it, as he was eating and drinking at the table; and besides he was paying little attention to the furniture, dulled as his senses were by fatigue, hunger, and the cold outside. He is, however, astonished not to have noticed what was then, as now, immediately facing him: the window, or at least the red curtains, made of a thin and shiny material that looks like satin.

These curtains could not have been closed; for as they are today, spread out in the full light, it is impossible not to be struck by their colour. So the window itself was probably visible, between two vertical red bands, very narrow, with not much light on them, and therefore much more discreet. But, if it was daylight, what did this window give out on? Was it a street-scene that was outlined in squares on the panes? In view of the monotony of the district such a sight would certainly not have been at all remarkable. Or else it was something else: a courtyard, perhaps so narrow, so dark at ground-floor level, that no particular light would come from it and nothing would attract the eye in that direction, especially if thick netting masked everything outside.

In spite of this reasoning the soldier is still bothered by such a lapse in his memory. He wonders if something else in his surroundings may have escaped him, and still escapes him even now. It suddenly seems to him very urgent to make a precise inventory of the room. There is the fireplace, of which he remembers almost nothing: an ordinary black marble fireplace, above which hangs a large rectangular mirror; the iron shutter is raised, a pile of grey, feathery ashes can be seen, but no fire-dogs; on the mantelpiece lies a fairly long object, not very high—only an inch or less at its highest part—which cannot be identified from this angle because it is not close enough to the edge of the marble (it may possibly even extend in width much further than it appears to); the mirror reflects the smooth, red satiny curtains, with vertical streaks of brightness on the folds. . . . The soldier has the impression that all this is nothing: in this room he should notice other details much more important than all these, one detail in particular, of which he was vaguely conscious when he entered here that other time, the day of the red wine and the slice of bread. . . . He cannot remember what is was. He wants to turn round to look more carefully in the direction of the chest of drawers. But he cannot move, except very slightly, a kind of numbness paralysing his whole body. Only his hands and forearms move with any ease.

'Is there anything you need?' the young woman asks in her deep voice.

Without changing her position she has stopped in the middle of her work, the knitting still held in front of her breast, the fingers still poised—one index raised, the other folded over—as if they were about to form another stitch, the face still lowered to make sure the stitch is properly executed, the eyes, however, raised towards the head of the bed. Her expression is solicitous, severe, still tense from concentrating on her work; or else from the anxiety this wounded man is causing her, turning up suddenly like this, or else for some other reason unknown to him.

'No,' he says, 'I don't need anything.'

He speaks slowly, in a way that surprises him, the words sounding abnormally detached from one another without his meaning to make them so.

'Does it hurt?'

'No,' he says. 'I can't . . . move . . . my body.'

'You mustn't move. If you need anything, ask me. It's because of the injection the doctor gave you. He will try and come again this evening to give you another one.' She has started knitting again, her eyes fixed on her work. 'If he can,' she goes on. 'You can't depend on anything now.'

It must also be the injection that produces this nausea which the soldier has felt since waking up. He is thirsty; but he does not want to get up to go and drink from the tap in the washroom at the end of the passage. He had better wait for the orderly in the canvas jacket and the hunting-boots to come back. No, that's not it: here it is the woman with the deep voice who is looking after him. It is only at this moment that he feels astonished at being once again in this room which belongs to a very much earlier scene. He clearly remembers the motorbike, the dark corridor where he lay down, sheltered, against the door. And then . . . He no longer knows what comes afterwards: not the hospital, probably, nor the crowded café, nor the long walk through the deserted streets, impossible now in his condition. He asks:

'The wound—is it serious?'

The woman goes on knitting as if she had not heard. He repeats:

'What sort of wound is it?'

He realises at this point that he is not speaking loudly enough, that he is shaping the words on his lips but not giving them enough breath. And yet, after the second time, the young woman has raised her head. She puts her work down on the table next to the big black ball of wool and remains quite still, staring at him in silence with a look of expectancy, or anxiety, or fear. At last she decides to ask:

'Did you say something?'

He repeats his question. This time the sounds, weak but distinct, do come out of his mouth, as if the voice with the too-low intonation were giving him back the use of his own voice; unless the woman guessed his words by lip-reading.

'No,' she says, 'It's nothing. It will soon be all over.'

'Getting up. . . .'

'No, not today. Nor tomorrow. A bit later.'

But he has no time to lose. He will get up this evening.

'The box,' he says '. . . where is it?'

To make himself understood he must begin the sentence again: 'The box . . . I had with me . . .'
A fleeting smile crosses the tense face:

'Don't worry about it—it's here. The lad brought it back. You mustn't talk so much. It'll hurt you.'

'No,' says the soldier. 'It doesn't hurt . . . too much.'

She has not picked up her knitting again; she goes on gazing at him with her two hands resting in her lap. She looks like a statue. The firm outline of her face with its regular features recalls that of the woman who served him wine one day, sometime, long ago. He makes an effort to say:

'I'm thirsty.'

His lips cannot even have moved for she does not get up or answer or make the slightest gesture. The pale eyes were in any case perhaps not even on him but on other drinkers sitting further away at other tables towards the other end of the room round which her eye continues to sweep, passing over the soldier and his two companions, now taking in the other tables along the wall where the small white notices are stuck up, each with four drawing pins, and the fine-printed text of which is still holding the attention of a knot of readers, now the front window covered up to eye-level with its gathered curtain and the three enamel balls in low relief on the outside of the pane, and the snow beyond, falling in slow, heavy, massed flakes with a uniform, vertical movement.

And the fresh layer thus gradually covering over the day's traces, rounding off the angles, filling in the dips, levelling the surfaces, has quickly effaced the

167

yellowish paths left along past the houses by the passers-by, the boy's isolated tracks, the two parallel furrows made by the motorcycle combination in the middle of the road.

But it must first be ascertained whether the snow is still falling. The soldier decides to ask the young woman. But would she know in this windowless room? She will have to go outside, through the door which is ajar, through the hall where the black umbrella is waiting and through the long succession of corridors, narrow stairs and more corridors again, turning at right angles and cutting across each other, and she might well get lost before reaching the street.

In any case she is taking a long time to come back and it is the boy who is now sitting in her place, at a slight angle to the table. He is wearing a roll-necked sweater, short trousers, woollen socks and felt slippers. He is sitting straight up without leaning against the back of the chair; his two arms are held stiffly at each side, the hands gripping the sides of the straw seat; his bare-kneed legs are swinging between the two front legs of the chair, executing in two parallel planes equal but opposite oscillations. When he notices the soldier looking at him he immediately stops his game; and as if he had been impatiently waiting for this moment to clear up a point that has been bothering him, he asks in his serious voice, which is not the voice of a child:

'Why are you here?'

'I don't know,' says the soldier.

The boy has probably not heard the answer for he puts his question again:

'Why didn't they send you to your barracks?'

The soldier cannot remember whether or not he has questioned the woman on this point. Obviously it was not the boy who carried him here, nor the disabled man. He must also ask whether anyone picked up the box wrapped in brown paper; the string was no longer holding and the parcel must have come undone.

'Are you going to die here?' says the boy.

The soldier does not know the answer to this question either. Moreover he is astonished that it should be asked. He will try and obtain an explanation; but he has not yet managed to formulate his anxieties when the boy turns and runs off at full speed along the rectilinear street, without even taking the time to swing round the cast-iron lampposts, passing them one after the other without stopping. Soon only his footprints are left in the level surface of the fresh snow, making a recognisable pattern, although distorted by his pace, then blurring more and more as that pace quickened, and finally becoming completely indistinct, impossible to follow among the other trails.

The young woman, for her part, has not moved from her chair; and she answers without being asked again, no doubt to keep the wounded man calm. It was the child who came to tell her that the soldier

169

she had looked after the day before was lying unconscious inside the entrance of a house a few streets
away, bent double, saying nothing, hearing nothing,
as still as if he were dead. She had at once decided to
go there. A man was already by the body, a civilian,
who had happened to be passing, he said, but who
seemed in fact to have witnessed the whole scene
from a distance, hidden in another doorway. She describes him without difficulty; an oldish man with
sparse grey hair, comfortably dressed with gloves,
spats and carrying an umbrella with an ivory knob.
This was lying on the floor across the threshold. The
door was wide open. The man was kneeling by the
wounded soldier, lifting an inert hand, holding the
wrist between his fingers to feel the strength of the
pulse; he was a doctor, more or less, although not
practising. It was he who had helped to carry the
body here.

As for the shoebox, the young woman had not
noticed its exact position, or even that it was there;
it must have been a little to the side, pushed out of
the way by the doctor so that he could carry out his
brief examination more easily. Although his con-
clusions had hardly been precise he had in any case
thought it preferable that the wounded man should
be put to bed in a comfortable place despite the risk
of transporting him without a stretcher.

But they had not set out at once because hardly
had the decision been taken when the noise of the
motorbike had started up again. The man had

quickly shut the door and they had waited in the dark for the danger to pass. The motorbike had come and gone several times, slowly patrolling the nearby streets, approaching, moving away, approaching again, but with its maximum intensity soon decreasing, each time, as it explored streets further and further off. When the noise was no more than a rumble, difficult to place, which they even had to listen for to hear with any certainty, the man reopened the door.

Everything was quiet all around. Nobody ventured into the streets any more now. In the still air a few sparse flakes of snow were falling. They lifted the body between them, the man holding it by the thighs and the woman by the shoulders, under the armpits. It was only then that she saw the spreading bloodstain on the side of the coat; but the doctor assured her it bore no relationship to the seriousness of the wound, and he stepped cautiously over the threshold carrying his part of the burden skilfully, followed by the young woman, more constrained, trying to keep the soldier in the position she thought would be lease uncomfortable for him, hardly able to manoeuvre this heavy body, adjusting her grip all the time, only managing to shake him up more. The boy, three steps ahead, had the silk-sheathed umbrella in one hand and the shoebox in the other.

The doctor then wanted to go home to fetch the wherewithal to give the necessary first aid to the wounded man, at least until a hospital could take him in (which might not be for some time, owing to the general chaos). But as they reached the young woman's house, which was fortunately very near, they heard once again the noise of engines, more muted though more powerful. This time it was not just motorbikes but large cars, or perhaps lorries. The man therefore had to wait for a while before venturing out. And they remained, all three of them, in the room where they had laid the still unconscious soldier on the divan. Standing quite still they gazed at him without saying a word, the woman near the bed-head, leaning forward slightly over the face, the man at the foot, still wearing his grey leather gloves and his fur-lined coat, the boy near the table in his cape and with his beret on his head.

The soldier has also remained fully clothed: coat, puttees and heavy boots. He is lying on his back with his eyes closed. He must be dead, for the others to leave him like that. And yet the following scene shows him in the bed with the sheets covering him up to the neck, half listening to a confused story which the same young woman with the light eyes is telling him: a sort of dispute that occurred between the kindly doctor with the grey gloves and a second person whom she does not clearly specify but who must be the disabled man. Apparently he had returned home—much later, after the first injection— and had wanted to do something which the other two were against, especially the doctor. Although the essence of their disagreement is not easy to disentangle, its violence is sufficiently obvious from the bearing of the opponents, who are letting fly with demonstrative gesticulations, theatrical attitudes and exaggerated posturings. The disabled man, who is leaning on the table with one hand, even goes so far as to brandish his crutch with the other; the doctor raises his arms to heaven with fingers open, like an inspired prophet teaching a new religion, or a Head of State acknowledging the cheering of the crowd. The woman, frightened by all this, steps aside to get away from the centre of the quarrel; but, without bringing up the foot which has remained behind, she turns her torso towards what she is avoiding, in order to follow the latest developments that may at any moment become dramatic, while at the same time hiding her eyes by spreading her hands out like a screen in front of her face. The boy is sitting on the floor, near an overturned chair; both his legs are stretched out on the ground, where they form a wide V; in his arms, tight against his chest, he holds the box wrapped in brown paper.

Then come other scenes, even less clear—even more deceptive, too, probably—violent, although for the most part they are silent. They are set in less precise, less distinctive, more impersonal places; a staircase keeps returning, several times; someone is coming down very briskly, holding the banister, missing out some of the steps, almost flying in a sort of spiral from one landing to another, while the soldier, to avoid being knocked down, is obliged to squeeze himself into a corner. Then he comes down himself, but more sedately, and at the end of the long corridor he comes out into the snow-covered street again; and at the end of the street he is back in the crowded café. All the characters are in their places: the proprietor behind the bar, the doctor in his fur-lined coat among the group of well-dressed men in the foreground, but standing a little apart from the others and not joining in their conversation, the child sitting on the floor beside a bench loaded with drinkers, near an overturned chair, still holding the box tightly in his arms, and the young woman in the gathered skirt, with the dark hair and the majestic bearing, holding her tray with its solitary bottle above the heads of the customers at the tables, and finally the soldier, sitting at the smallest table between his two companions, mere foot-soldiers like himself, and like him wearing coats buttoned up to the collar and forage caps, as tired as he is, seeing nothing—no more than he—around them, holding themselves as stiffly on their chairs as he is doing, and like him remaining silent. All three have exactly the same face; the only difference between them is that one is seen in left profile, the other in full face, the third in right profile; and their arms are folded in the same way, their six hands resting in the same way on the table, over which the chequered oilcloth falls at each corner in rigid, conical folds.

Is it from this frozen group that the waitress is turning away towards the right, showing the profile of a classical statue, but with her body already facing the other way towards the well-dressed man who is standing slightly behind his own group, seen in profile also and from the same side, with features as motionless as hers, as theirs? Another character also remains impassive among the contortions of the crowd around him; this is the child, sitting on the floor in the foreground, on the chevroned parquet that is like that of the room itself, continuing it, so to speak, beyond a short separation consisting of the vertical section of striped wallpaper and, lower down, the three drawers of the chest of drawers.

The chevroned parquet goes on beyond that, without any other interruption, as far as the heavy red curtains, at the top of which the filiform shadow of the fly is continuing its circuit on the white ceiling, passing now near the crack that spoils the uniformity of the surface near the angle of wall and ceiling, in the right-hand corner, within the direct line of vision of the person lying on the divan, his neck supported by the bolster.

It would be necessary to get up in order to see from closer up exactly what this fault consists of: is it really a crack, or a cobweb, or something quite different? One would very likely have to climb on a chair, or even on a step-ladder.

But, once up, other thoughts would quickly get in the way of that particular project: the soldier would thus first have to find the shoebox, which has probably been put away in another room, in order to go and deliver it to the person for whom it is meant. Since this is out of the question for the time being, the soldier can only stay where he is, flat on his back, his head supported slightly by the bolster, staring straight in front of him.

And yet his mind feels clearer, less sleepy, despite the persistent nausea and the increasing numbness of his whole body which has worsened since the second injection. It seems to him that the young woman leaning over him to make him drink is looking at him with greater anxiety.

She is speaking to him again about the disabled man, against whom she seems to feel some sort of grudge, or even hatred. Several times already she has mentioned this man who shares her home, and always with a mixture of reticence and of the need on the contrary to explain herself on this point, as if she were ashamed of this presence, seeking at one and the same time to justify it, destroy it, and forget it. And the young woman never specifies the precise relationship that links them. She has had to struggle, among other things, to prevent the man from opening the shoebox; he had said it was absolutely essential to know what it contained. And she had even wondered herself what they should do about it. . . .

'Nothing,' says the soldier. 'I'll take care of it as soon as I'm up.'

'But,' she says, 'if it's important, and you had to stay a long time. . . .'

She suddenly looks as if she is seized with genuine anguish, for which the soldier feels himself responsible and which he would like to alleviate.

'No,' he says, 'it isn't all that important.'

'But what should we do with it?'

'I don't know.'

'Were you looking for someone? Did you have to give it to him?'

'Not necessarily; to him or someone else he would have told me about.'

'And for him, was it important?'

'Could have been. I'm not sure.'

'But what's in it?'

She has spoken this last sentence so vehemently that he feels obliged to inform her as far as he can, despite the exhaustion this conversation is causing him, despite the scant interest he himself has on this particular point, despite his fear of disappointing her by the insignificance of his answer:

'Nothing much, I think. I didn't look. Letters probably, papers, personal things.'

'Did it belong to a friend?'

'No, a comrade, I hardly knew him.'

'Did he die?'

'Yes, in the hospital, he was wounded, in the belly.'

'And it was important to him?'

'I expect so. He'd asked for me, I arrived too late, a few minutes. They gave me the box on his behalf.

Then someone telephoned for him. I took the call. His father, I think, or not quite. They didn't have the same name. I wanted to know, what to do, with the box.'

'And he arranged to meet you.'

Yes; the man on the telephone arranged the meeting in his own town, this one, which the soldier was to try and reach, now that it was everyone for himself, with the army in full flight. The place of the rendezvous was not the man's home, for family reasons or something of that sort, but in the street, for all the cafés were closing one after another. The soldier found an army lorry transporting old uniforms which was going that way. But he had to do some of the journey on foot.

He did not know the town. He may have mistaken the spot. It was at the intersection of two perpendicular streets, near a lamp-post. He had not heard very well or had not remembered the names of the streets. He had relied on the topographical directions, following the prescribed route as best he could. When he thought he had arrived he waited. The crossroads looked like the description given, but the name did not tally with the vague sound he had memorised. He waited a long time. He saw nobody.

He was sure of the day at any rate. As for the time, he had no watch. Perhaps he arrived too late. He searched the neighbouring streets. He waited again at another crossroads identical to the first. He wandered through the whole district. He went back several times to the first place, at least in so far as he was able to recognise it, that day and the following days. It was in any case too late by then.

'A few minutes only. He had just died, without anyone noticing. I had stayed in a café with some N.C.O.s, some strangers. I didn't know. They told me to wait for a friend, someone else, a conscript. He was at Reichenfels.'

'Which one was at Reichenfels?' the woman asks.

She leans a little further towards the bed. Her deep voice fills the whole room as she insists:

'Who? What regiment was he in?'

'I don't know. Another man. The doctor was there too, with his grey ring, leaning against the counter. And the woman, the disabled man's wife perhaps, serving wine.'

'What are you talking about?'

Her face is close to his. Her pale eyes, darkly ringed, are made larger still by the widening of the eyelids.

'Must go and fetch the box,' he says. 'It must still be at the barracks. I'd forgotten it. It's on the bed, behind the bolster. . . .'

'Now relax. Lie quiet. Don't try and talk any more.'

She stretches out her hand to pull up the sheet. On the palm and the inside of the fingers are black marks like paint or grease which washing has not removed.

179

'Who are you?' says the soldier. 'What should I call you? What name? . . .'

But she does not seem to hear any more. She arranges the sheets and the pillow, tucks in the blanket.

'Your hand . . .' continues the soldier. This time he can go no further.

'Relax,' she says. 'It's nothing. It's from carrying you. The coat had fresh stains on the sleeve.'

They stumble at each step in the soft earth lined with transverse furrows and ridges, in the darkness that is lit up now and then with fleeting glows. They have both abandoned their packs. The wounded man has also left his rifle behind. But he has kept his; its strap has just given way so that he has to carry the gun by the middle, horizontally, in his hand. The boy, three paces ahead, is carrying the umbrella in the same way. The wounded man becomes heavier and heavier and hangs round the soldier's neck, making his progress even more difficult. Now he cannot move at all; neither his arms nor even his head. He can only look straight ahead of him, at the leg of the table, from which the oilcloth has been removed, at the table-leg now visible up to the top: it ends in a ball topped by a cube, or rather an almost cubic parallelepiped, square in the horizontal section but a little larger in the vertical; the vertical face is decorated with a pattern carved in the wood within a rectangular frame that follows the outline of the face itself, a sort of stylised flower with a straight stem and at the top two small symmetrical arches diverging on either side, like a V with its arms curving over, bending down, a little shorter than the terminal portion of the axial stem, from the same point, and . . . the eyes cannot remain lowered so long and must move up the long red curtains, soon coming to the ceiling again, and the crack, thin as a hair, just slightly winding, it too so precise and complicated in shape that one would have to follow it with great attention, concentrating hard on its bends, its curves, its wobbles and uncertainties, its sudden changes of direction, crooks, straightenings, slight retreats, but one would need more time, a little time, a few minutes, a few seconds, and it is already, now, too late.

At my last visit there was no need for the third injection. The wounded soldier was dead. The streets are full of armed soldiers marching past to rhythmic songs, sung at a low pitch, more nostalgic than gay. Open lorries go by full of men sitting up stiffly, rifles held rigidly at the vertical with both hands between their knees; they sit in two rows, back to back, each row facing one side of the street. Patrols are everywhere and nobody is allowed to go out after nightfall without a pass. However, the third injection had to be given and only an authorised doctor could have got permission to go. Luckily the streets were badly lit, certainly much worse lit than in the last few days when the electricity was on even in full daylight. As for the injection, however, it was too late. In any case their only purpose was to make the dying man's last hours less painful. Nothing else could be done.

The body is still at the 'disabled' man's place. He will make a formal statement, telling the whole story as it really happened: a wounded man they found in the street, whose name they did not even know since he had no papers on him. If the man is afraid that if he does it his leg will be examined and his actual condition discovered, the woman can take charge of the formalities; as for him, he need only keep out of sight when they come to fetch the body; it will not be the first time he has hidden from a visitor.

The woman seems to distrust him. At any rate she did not want to let him take charge of the parcel wrapped in brown paper, although he very much wanted to open it. He thought it was some secret weapon, or at least the plans for one. The box is now quite safe—on the black marble, which is cracked, of the chest of drawers—re-closed, re-wrapped, re-tied. But bringing it back here from their place was not easy with all the patrols around. It was not far, fortunately.

Just before the end of the journey a brief order rang out: 'Halt!' shouted in a loud voice, some distance behind. The box itself was not particularly compromising, as might have been imagined; the suspicions of the 'disabled' man on this subject were of course absurd, but the woman had nevertheless been afraid that the letters mentioned by the soldier might contain something other than personal information, something of military or political interest for instance, the soldier himself having at all times been exaggeratedly discreet as to their nature. It was better, in any case, not to let them be confiscated, all the more so because the bayonet that the woman had handed over at the same time could, in the event, look very suspect indeed. The absence of a pass would have made the bearer's case worse still. The loud, imperious voice shouted 'Halt!' a second time, then a third, and immediately a machine-gun rattled off a few brief salvoes. But it must have been too far to aim correctly, and it was very dark at that spot. They may even have been shooting in the air. Once round the corner of the street there was no further danger. The door of the building had not been left ajar, naturally. But the key turned noiselessly in the lock, the hinges did not squeak, the door closed silently.

The letters, at first glance, contain no secret of any kind, or anything of the slightest general or personal importance. They are ordinary letters, such as a country girl might send each week to her fiancé, giving him news of the farm or of the neighbours, regularly repeating the same conventional phrases about separation and reunion. The box also contains an ancient gold watch of no great value, with a brass chain that has lost its gilt; no name is engraved inside the cover over the watch-face; and a ring, a signet ring made of silver or nickel alloy such as workers often make for themselves in the factory, and inscribed 'H.M.'; lastly, a short dagger or bayonet, of the current model, identical to the one handed over by the young woman together with the parcel, and of which she had been unwilling to divulge the source, saying merely that she was afraid of keeping it in view of the new orders about the surrender of weapons, but that she nevertheless did not want to hand it in (it was the 'disabled' man, no doubt, who insisted on her getting rid of it). The box is not a shoebox; it is a biscuit-box; similar in size, but made of tin.

The most important things of all are the envelopes of the letters: they bear the name—Henri Martin— of the soldier to whom they were addressed, and his field post-office number. On the back is the name and address of the girl who wrote them. The whole thing will have to be sent to her when the post office is working again, since it is now impossible to trace the father, who is not even named Martin. In any case it was probably only for reasons of convenience that he agreed provisionally to receive the parcel: even if he knew the contents of the box he thought he would be geographically easier to reach than the fiancée herself. Unless the letters alone are meant for her, the dagger-bayonet, the watch and the ring belonging by right to the father. It is also possible that even the letters were not intended to be returned to their sender; innumerable reasons could easily be put together to support this thesis.

Rather than send the parcel through the post it would probably be better to deliver it in person, with the conventional tactful phrases. The girl might after all not have been told yet about her fiancé's death. Only the father was told, when he rang up the hospital; and if he is not the real father—or not the legal father, or in some way not wholly the father— he may well have no contact with the girl, or even no knowledge of her existence; there is thus no reason why he should write to her when the postal services are working again.

The woman who looked after the wounded soldier obtained no information from him about the comrade who died before him. He talked a great deal towards the end, but he had already forgotten the greater part of recent events; and anyway he was delirious more often than not. The woman swears that he was already ill before he was wounded, that he was feverish and behaved at times like a sleep-walker. Her son, a child of about ten with a serious face, had met him before in the street, perhaps even several times, if at any rate it really is the same boy each time, as seems likely despite some small incon-sistencies. His is a fundamental role since it is he, out of sheer carelessness, who set off the action of the occupants of the motorcycle combination, but his numerous appearances are not all so important. The disabled man, on the other hand, plays practically no

185

part. There is nothing surprising about his daily presence at the military offices in the rue Bouvet, converted into a sick-bay or reception centre, in view of the ease with which he moved when no one was watching him. Moreover, the soldier does not seem to have paid much attention to what he said.

The café proprietor, for his part, is enigmatic, or insignificant. He does not say a single word or make a single gesture; this large bald man may just as well be a spy or a police informer, it being impossible to determine the nature of his thoughts. The extras who argue before him so animatedly will in any case teach him nothing worth reporting to his bosses, if he has any; they are mere café tacticians who remake history to suit themselves, criticising ministers, correcting the actions of generals, creating imaginary episodes that would have made possible, among other things the winning of the battle of Reichenfels. The soldier sitting at the last table but one, at the back on the right, certainly has a more realistic view of the fighting, which means he has nothing to say to them; he is probably only waiting to be served, between his two companions whose faces are not entirely visible, the one being in profile and the other seen from the rear quarter. His first change of uniform can be explained by the general scorn, no doubt unjustified, in which his regiment has been held since the defeat; he has judged it preferable, before undertaking his journey, to wear less noticeable badges.

In this way he can mingle with the crowd in the café without attracting attention, and quietly drink the wine the waitress is about to give him. Meanwhile he stares ahead of him through the large front window. The snow has stopped falling. The weather has turned slowly milder during the day. The pavements are still white but the road, where the lorries have been ceaselessly passing for hours, is already black again down the middle, with piles of half-melted snow pushed back towards the gutters on either side; each time the soldier crosses a transverse street he sinks in up to his puttees with a squelch, as the sparse drops of a fine drizzle begin to float in the evening air, still mingled with a few wet flakes which turn into water before they reach the street.

The soldier is reluctant to leave the crowded café into which he has come to rest for a moment. It is the rain he is gazing at, outside the large window, beyond the gathered curtain and the three billiard balls in low relief. It is also the rain that the child is watching, sitting on the floor, right up against the window so that he can see through the thin net curtain. The downpour grows in violence. The rolled umbrella in its black silk sheath is leaning against the coat-stand, near the fur-lined coat. But in the engraving so many other clothes are hanging with it, heaped on top of one another, that it is difficult to distinguish anything at all in the pile. Immediately below the picture is the chest of drawers with its three highly polished drawers each bearing two large knobs of tarnished brass. In the bottom drawer is the biscuit-box wrapped in brown paper. The rest of the room is unchanged: the ashes in the fireplace, the sheets of paper scattered over the table, the cigarette ends filling the glass ashtray to the brim, the lighted desk-lamp, the heavy red curtains hermetically closed.

Outside it is raining. Outside in the rain one has to walk with head bent, hand shielding eyes that peer ahead nevertheless, a few yards ahead, a few yards of wet asphalt. Here the rain does not enter, nor does the snow, nor the wind; and the only fine dust that dulls the shine of the horizontal planes, the varnished table-top, the polished chevroned parquet, the marble of the mantelpiece, the cracked marble of the chest of drawers, the only dust here comes from the room itself, from the gaps in the parquet possibly, or from the bed, or the ashes in the fireplace, or the velvet curtains whose vertical folds reach from the floor to the ceiling where the shadow of the fly—the shape of the glowing filament of the electric bulb that is hidden by the conical lamp-shade—is now passing the thin black line which, as it is in the darkness beyond the circle of light, and some twenty feet away, can only very vaguely be guessed at: a short segment to the right, first, less than half an inch long, followed by a series of rapid undulations, themselves festooned . . . but the eye mists up as it tries to chart the course of the line, as with the too-fine pattern of the wallpaper and the uncertain outlines of the gleaming paths traced in the dust by the felt slippers, and, beyond the door of the room, the dark hall where the umbrella is leaning at an angle against the coat-stand, then, once past the front door, the succession of long corridors, the spiral stair-case, the door of the building with its stone step, and the whole town behind me.